To Helena: —
I hope you enjoy
these stories,

Will Gorb葛
林

LOVE IN BEIJING
AND OTHER STORIES

BY

WILLIAM GOEDE

CORMORANT BOOKS

Summit, Forbidden City and *The Pilgrim* have appeared in *Canadian Fiction Magazine; Porgy and Bess and Sung Li* has appeared in *Canadian Forum.*

The publisher wishes to acknowledge the support of The Canada Council and The Ontario Art Council.

Typeset in Dunvegan by Greenglass Graphics. Printed in Winnipeg by Hignell.

Cover from a Chinese ceramic tile made in Xian.

Published by Cormorant Books, RR 1, Dunvegan, Ontario, Canada K0C 1J0

Canadian Cataloguing in Publication Data

Goede, William
    Love in Beijing and other stories

ISBN 0-920953-42-5

    I. Title.

PS8563.O819L69 1988   C813' .54   C88-090378-3
PR9199.3.G64L69 1988

CONTENTS

For Marilyn Goede,
who knows all about the Forbidden City

PREFACE

Ritter arrived at the hotel in the dead of night. They helped him carry his trunk to his rooms and told him they'd be back tomorrow to take him for a ride around town and then out to a banquet at the Language Institute thrown by the president and the Party leader.

The rooms were badly lit. He could scarcely find his way around. He walked slowly with hands held out before him as he navigated between the toilet and the coffin-long bedroom, where he found twin beds, one of which had had the silk coverlets laid back for him. He went to the window and gazed down into the yellow street, which at that hour of night rang with horses and carts bearing high heaps of the most unusual goods. They looked like ghosts superimposed upon makebelieve trees that lined a storybook road, and their bells flew up and echoed through the long empty rooms. It all seemed like a dream.

When he woke in the morning it was all still there. He dressed and walked down the stairs and out into the court-yard. It didn't look like any hotel he had ever seen in his life. It was straight out of the 1950s— the old, square windows, the whitewashed trees and box hedges lining the walks, and up above the grey walls and dark windows, the tile roofs. He wandered out of the courtyard and into the road that curved out and around the hotel grounds. It separated the massive five-storey ornate stone structures clustered about the huge square and the burnt-out shell of a Chinese Theatre from the proletarian four-storey grey-brick structures, all of which were photocopies of each other. The road was cordoned with mighty trees shedding their broadleaf foliage and filtering in the orange autumnal morning sun that played across his skin and made him seem like someone he had never met before. Chinese workers passed him with scarcely a glance, as if they hadn't seen him. Perhaps he was invisible.

He walked twice around the circle road before he met the man in white. He was a tall, athletic man with grey mutton-chops and clad in a white peasant blouse and a white hat that reminded Ritter of the ones that Frank Lloyd Wright used to wear. He decided to follow the man in white. The man led him to The Number Eight Dining Room, a huge, fashionable room nearly empty. The man in white joked in Chinese with a waiter and then beckoned Ritter to join him, and before breakfast was over he had met almost all the foreigners who lived in the hotel. This was where they were kept, like lions in a zoo.

Ritter went back to his room and thought about them. He had come out to China to enquire deeply into the mysteries of this most ancient of civilizations— and enquire he would, finding the mysteries were even more mysterious and wonderful than in his wildest imagination. But what puzzled him even more were the inhabitants of this sad grey hotel on the outskirts of the city. In fact, he spent most of the year observing them. They wouldn't go away. He tried to dismiss them, and when they wouldn't go away, he'd pack a suitcase, go down to the train station and buy a ticket for Xian, but just as soon as he got snug and warm in his soft-seat sleeper compartment, he would get out his journal and sift through his thoughts in hopes of making sense out of them. He was not a writer, but he became one in writing about them.

China was, indeed, a wonderful place and he came to love these strange Chinese people he served; but far stranger were the people in his own hotel. He became obsessed with observing them. In this way Ritter felt akin to the Chinese, who described themselves as the most intelligent and creative people in the world and yet they, too, had become obsessed, ever since The Downfall of the Gang of Four, with the examination of these foreigners who had conquered the

8

world while their backs were turned. They knew they themselves had been navel-gazing ever since the Ming Dynasty. They knew they had squandered their advantage. They had somehow come to believe that they were superior to these foreigners, and divine. They had forgotten the cardinal rule of history, that once you think you've got it all, you've lost it.

Ritter began to sketch the foreigners at the hotel one at a time, but they had a way of sneaking into the other stories, and so let them have their way. Some were a bigger mystery to him than others, and it took longer to tell their story. But they all wanted to talk . Ritter went mad hearing all their voices all the time. They simply would not sit still.

LOVE IN BEIJING

1

Hagstrom only talks about it when he's good and drunk.

He stumbles around the room talking to himself and before you know it, he's back at the window again and leaning over the sill and meditating out loud about the *fuwuyuan* gathered together on the benches in front of his doorway drinking green tea and giggling and reading old yellow newspapers. Something about these young room clerks and how they're the front line of the Chinese secret service, and you have to suppress a giggle of disbelief as you gaze across the tidal blue tile roofs and arcane brick walls and deep into the heart of Coleridge's Xanadu and Mao's Forbidden City. You know he's only warming up so he can tell the story to you once more.

Finally he says, "He was just out of college and his old man had given him a return ticket to Hongkong as a graduation present."

This is the way it starts. Different words maybe, but built out over the same quicksand, and when he talks, his eyes glaze over and he gets down to the tonic of his voice. "He had worked at this hamburger stand in Edmonton and saved every penny he earned and so he decided on the spur of the moment to take a little side trip up to Beijing. It was all very innocent, you know. He checked out of his hotel and went down to Tian'anmen Square and walked straight into her." There is something behind all the words that brings out the darkness in his voice. "She stood there blocking his path,

stood square in the middle of the sidewalk and right below
The Chairman's portrait speaking English at him and intro-
ducing him to her classmates and her teacher, a pale, shy
older woman in a faded Mao jacket who bent her head slightly
and smiled coldly up at him. The girl told him her name was
Xiao Li but he could call her Little Lily or just plain Lily if he
wanted to because that was what they called her in her
English classes."

"I don't see what he sees in her," I say, sourly. I had
passed Derek Usher and Xiao Li in the dark hotel passageways and though they seemed pleasant enough, I found them
shy, distant, plain, even a little boring. They were friends of
Hagstrom's, and, like him, reclusive, and inclined to hysteria
and paranoia. "Her eyes are too far apart and she shows her
teeth when she talks."

"It is not for you to judge," says Hagstrom, rolling his
fat rubber belly along the window sill as if trying to inflate
himself. "We're talking about love, Ritter. We're talking
about the occult. You see, Derek was just a hirsuit post-
hippy hippy. He had been too late for love-ins and Haight-
Ashbury but just in time for dope and dropping-out. He had
just graduated from university and his little bit of knowledge
proved to be more than dangerous. He had mastered the art
of stock futures and Sybex 1-2-3 and had also taken some
courses in oriental history and gotten a couple A's in them,
and so when his father told him he had given him a return
ticket to Thailand as a graduation gift, he went to a Head
Shop and bought a Lonely Planet guidebook on The Golden
Triangle and headed for Hongkong and Chiang Mai and the
Hill Tribes who, it was said, kept you stoned for months. But
he was a little disappointed. The "highs" he experienced were
less related to the black, oily opium his hosts rolled up for
him than in walking through the dust motes of dawn in a
town that was a still life of the stone age. He wasn't in any
hurry to get back to Edmonton either, because he didn't have
a job back there and the likelihood was he'd never get one or
if he did, it'd be that of a part-time parking-lot attendant
who'd spend his nights holed up alone in a hot, dry tomblike
kiosk until some drunk slicked out on VO5 and prune juice

slipped up on him and shot him between the eyes.

"He found his way to Beijing eventually, where he met a couple other hirsuit college students who had already decided to go back home and take that job in the parking lot, and after tooling around Beijing for a week with them, decided to follow them out to Hongkong. He didn't really want to leave China because something had touched him very deep, something he didn't quite understand. Maybe it was the people and maybe the intensity of their relationships; maybe it was their capacity to endure the weight of centuries and dynasties; maybe it was their simple laughter, because, you see, in spite of his dirty beard and long hair and big nose, they had come out of their holes and even out of the safety of their language to talk to him and show him they were people, too."

"You got to be kidding," I say, sneeringly.

"He figured he hadn't got the message yet."

"So he decided to sleep with one of them and find out what it was. The message, that is."

Hagstrom pours himself another glass of beer and falls heavily into his chair. He isn't going to listen to me anymore. So I sit before him and adopt the usual skeptical body expressions I use whenever he gets into one of his story-making moods. He stares at the open window as if to show me he doesn't care one way or the other what I do with my body. "I take it," he says, "she was a little scared when he showed up at her school the next day and told her he wasn't going back to Edmonton but instead had taken a room in a dormitory hotel and was out looking for a job."

2

She listened politely to him and then told him she would walk him back to the gate. She tiptoed along beside him as they walked between the dull brick dormitories of the Language Institute like someone carrying a time bomb into the street.

The students who passed her on the sidewalk told her with their eyes she would have a lot of explaining to do when she got back. At the gate she refused to look the foreigner in the eyes as she told him it had all been a horrible mistake and he should return to Canada as soon as possible and forget everything that had happened and that there would be trouble if he stayed. Derek Usher considered her words for a while and then calmly informed her he would wait for her in Tian'anmen Square the following Sunday at three in the afternoon, and if she didn't come, he might have to come back out to her school again to look for her. His persistence did not frighten her half so much as the eyes of the old gateman who stared at the two of them from his broken stool, and so she said, more to get rid of him, that she would try to make it to Tian'anmen on Sunday. He said nothing at all about his feelings for her, but, as they parted, she could see something in his eyes that spoke past words and around translation, and she knew she was in deep trouble.

When she returned, she found Zhang tongzhi before the door of her dormitory.

"What have you done?" he said, breathlessly.

She was amazed at herself. She was not afraid, she hadn't flinched. And for some reason she remembered the summer of 1966. She was just a girl in 1966. She and her comrades had just finished pillaging an old woman's apartment on the third floor of a tenement house in the Xidan District and had carried the Four Olds down from it and piled them up for burning. The old woman herself came down with tears in her eyes and told her that she had gone to an international conference in Budapest in 1955 with Premier Zhou and could she maybe just keep one picture of herself standing with him, please, and so Xiao Li pulled a picture from the burning pile of goods and gave it to her. One of her comrades snarled at her for it, and Xiao Li said, "Comrade Zhou is not an enemy of the people!" But they refused to see it that way, and afterward she had had to attend a struggle session and admit she had been wrong.

"You must not see this foreign friend again," said Zhang.

"Why should you worry?" she said, controlling her anger. "We have done nothing wrong. There is no *guiding*

against seeing foreign friends. It is part of our modernization. Lao Dong herself took the class to Tian'anmen to speak
to foreign friends."

"You will get your comrade teacher into trouble."

"I am sorry for that."

"And you will get me into trouble, too."

She stared at him, waiting for him to say more, but he
retreated to his cold little room, where a lukewarm cup of
green tea and a week-old *China Daily* lay on his desk.

She got to Tian'anmen an hour before Derek Usher. He came
clean-shaven and with a regulation Chinese haircut and he
wore a blue cotton Mao jacket. He was smiling like a boy
Buddha as he walked up to her.

"I have a job at the Youdianxueyuan!" he said, mas-
ticating on a word he had been practicing all week. "I went
out to the Friendship Hotel and talked to a bunch of teachers
and found out that a foreign expert at the Youdianxueyuan
had just gone home sick and they were looking for someone
to take her place."

"Aiye!" she said.

He smiled and stared up past Xiao Li's pigtails and
into the blank gaze of Chairman Mao, who, Derek figured,
was purposefully studying the bright horizon of man's future
so as to avoid prying into their private affairs. "I want you to
teach me Chinese," he said. "Will you do it?"

She laughed and said, "If you will teach me English."

And they found a lot more to laugh about that afternoon as they walked slowly across the hot cobblestone cul-
de-sac courtyards of the purple emperors of the dragon
kingdom. They even laughed when they tried to pry their way
up into the great wall of bodies packed solidly inside the
number 15 bus in Wangfujinglu. He rode all the way out to
her institute, and she said when he got out that she didn't
want him walking her to the gate because now she was going
to have to learn how to be discreet.

But those who were looking had seen him, and when
she strolled through the gates, Lao Wang, who usually smiled
at her and joked about the time she blew up one of the tires

14

on her bicycle at the pump, called out to her.

"Lao Zhang," he said, looking at the ground, "wants to see you in his office." She got her bicycle and rode to the classroom building and, as she dismounted, they came out and Zhang spoke to her. She listened to him without saying a word, and when he was finished speaking, he turned without saying *zaijian* and walked back into the building. The others stood and watched her. She got back on her bicycle and rode to her dormitory and told her classmates what Zhang had said.

She told Derek about it, too. "I must not talk you about these troubles," she said, trying to brighten. They walked through the busiest part of Tian'anmen and into the shade of the monolith of the People's Heroes, where they sat. "You will become angry," she said, the words pitching into her mouth with amazing accuracy. There was something about this man that inspired her to speak English in a way none of her teachers had ever been able to do. It seemed now as if she had been born to speak English. She studied the foreigner's face and found in its planes of light the beauty, strength and honesty she had been seeking all her life. She liked the bright, copper color of his hair and the depth of his blue eyes, the strength of forehead, the square conviction of his chin. "I wish you speak to me about your family and your way of life," she said. "I wish you speak everything about you." She laughed, but tears came to her eyes. "They cannot stop me. I meeting you and hearing you."

He was head-over-heels in love with this girl. He almost cried too when she spoke, and to mask his feelings, he coughed and stared at the high dragon kites flying above the square, wishing that he and Xiao Li, too, could soar above a world so deeply divided.

"I do not want you to get into trouble for me," he said. "I have been unfair. I would feel very bad if I got you into trouble."

She tried to laugh again. "There are many bad people at language institute," she said, "but many good people, too. Good people understand and follow new policy. Everything change now. We modernizing. We take place in the world. The old men, they cannot go back to the old days." She stared at him. "They cannot stop us."

"Xiao Li," he said, "I must tell you in honesty that I really love you." She looked away, reddened. "I am trying not to insult you. I will not even talk about how I really feel about you, but I must say I really do love you."

"No," she said, getting up, "do not talk such things now." They walked around the Mao mausoleum to Qianmen. "We will talk of these things later." After a while she said, "Next Sunday, we will visit my home. I have already written letter. We will meet here eight o'clock in the morning. We will take a train." They walked slowly through the crowds of pilgrims in from the countryside, and he had to fight aside a desire to hold her hand, and when at last they returned to the very place they had met, she turned to smile at him with the most beautiful eyes he had ever seen.

"I must go now. *Zaijian*, Derek."

"*Zaijian*, Xiao Li."

He had gone straight back to his institute.

But she, it seems, had taken but a few steps when two men she had never seen before blocked her path and told her she was coming with them.

3

They sent her to a shoe factory in Jinan, deep in the province of Shandong. It was for her own good.

She wrote him from Jinan to explain why she wasn't in the square to take him out to meet her parents and said she expected to be at the shoe factory for no longer than one year and then she would write the examination again and hopefully return to the Second Foreign Language Institute in Beijing. She had been foolish. She asked him to forget her and to go about his business, and from time to time she would write. She asked him not to write to her because they would never allow her to receive letters from him. Still, she enclosed her address in English and in Chinese and sent a small picture her classmates had taken of her so that he could remember what she looked like.

Derek had no idea where Jinan was but he went

anyway.

It turned out to be an overnight train ride. When he arrived in the dark and sleeping city at four in the morning, he walked into the station and pulled out his tiny English-Chinese guide. "*Chu zu chi che zai nali?*" he said, but the man merely stared at him with the expression of a man who had just heard a monkey talk. Derek repeated himself but nothing happened. The man only continued staring at him. So he walked out into the street and said the same words to somebody else, but this time the man fled. He tried it several times with similar results.

After a while he pulled out Xiao Li's letter and showed a man the address she had written out in Chinese, and the man smiled and tried to speak to him. Derek understood nothing, but together they walked and talked until at last the man pointed to a set of dusty, grey factory buildings. Derek shook his hand feverishly, and the man ducked away from him like a man escaping an avalanche.

"*Ni zao!*" he said to the sleepy gate-keeper. "*Wo shii Usher laoshi,*" he said, having practiced his little speech all the way down from Beijing. "*Wo yao Li Mailing tongzhi can-guan.*" The old man stared at him for a while and then launched forth in a stream of sounds, but Derek had no idea what he said. He dug out his traveller's dictionary and sought feverishly for more words, but the old man disappeared, and he was left standing there at the gate. He waited for a half-hour, but the old man did not return. He went over to a bench just outside the gate and dropped his backpack on it, sat and waited.

He refused to leave. Two hours later a man approached him and smiled down at him with the eyes of a man who had drawn the short straw and lost. "Good morning," he said. "My name Mr. Sung. I sorry I cannot be early. You see, I sorry."

Derek got to his feet and shook his hand. "Don't worry," he said. "I am visiting a friend of mine. She works in your factory. Her name is Li Mailing. Do you know her?"

"Perhaps, I not sure," he said. "But you see, it not possible you see her now." Derek waited, but Sung offered no explanation. "You return Beijing. I go now to train station, buy ticket to you."

"No," said Derek. "I am not going back unless I talk with Xiao Li."

"But, you see, it not possible."

"Why?"

"She not here."

"Where is she?"

"She gone."

"Where?"

He smiled. "You see, I not know."

Mr. Sung was the very spirit of international understanding in the car going back to the train station. *Bai qiu en dai fu.* Dr. Norman Bethune. The bells had been sounded. Also, he had been to Toronto once. He loved Canada. China and Canada were friends. Canadian friends were helping to modernize the Motherland. Mr. Sung even shook hands inside the soft sleeper car before he left Derek and explained that it had been a real pleasure meeting him and that it might not be a good idea to return.

He wrote to Xiao Li when he got home, but no letters came for him. So, on the following Friday he once again took the overnight train to Jinan and by early morning light again had a short, fruitless conversation with the sleepy old man at the gate who once more fetched the effervescent Mr. Sung from some distant sanctuary to make all the suitable excuses.

"Good morning! Good morning!" he said, grasping Derek's hands like an old friend. "Very nice see you again."

"Nice to see you," said Derek. This time he had brought a jug of hot water and two tea cups, and the two of them sat in the rising sun and drank tea together on the bench, while the old man watched from his apple box seat at the gate. "I want to talk to Xiao Li," he said. "Can you take me to see her?"

"No, no, quite not possible!" smiled Mr. Sung.

"Why is that?"

"She busy."

"Busy?"

"Yes, she working in fields."

"But this is a shoe factory."

"Much work in fields. You see, she work in fields. It far from here."

"When will she return?"

"Monday. She come Monday back."

"I will wait until Monday."

Mr. Sung laughed anxiously. "But, you see," said Mr. Sung, dropping his voice into a confession, "she not see you because she go work."

"You are telling me I may never see her?"

"Oh, no!" laughed Mr. Sung. Derek had gone too far. He was being unfriendly. "But, you see, now very difficult."

Derek stared at the old man at the gate, who, it seemed, understood their conversation without knowing one word of it.

Derek went back to Beijing empty-handed again, but he was back the following weekend as well, and though Xiao Li was unavailable, this time because of political meetings, he made a promise to Mr. Sung, that he would return every weekend until he was able to see her. On his ride back to Beijing, he realized for the first time that he loved her more than he had ever loved anyone in his life and for no apparent reason. He was a little worried because he figured he might have misconstrued a high sense of justice and anger for love and yet he decided that if they refused the next time to bring her to him, he would go inside the factory to look for her.

4

He didn't have to do anything too awful the next time because she was waiting for him just inside the gate. She stood like a statue before him, the courtyard behind her a sea of old people moving gracefully to the cackling martial music of a loudspeaker, a blue tai qi chorus line glancing from time to time at the three of them as if they symbolized something. Mr. Sung stood quietly at attention beside, and slightly behind, Xiao Li, and when she spoke, he looked away.

"You must not see me more," she said slowly. She

avoided his eyes. She looked at the ground. "I must not see you more. This is goodbye."

The way she held herself belied all this, and Derek knew when she spoke, it was Mr. Sung's words in her mouth. He hadn't seen Xiao Li for two months. She was more beautiful than he remembered, and sadder: her neon-black hair wreathed, her dark eyes established, the broad cheeks glistening.

"I cannot believe you mean it." Derek looked at Mr. Sung, who had found something of interest in a window on the far side of the compound. Perhaps it was his own ventriloquist. "I think it is a lie." If he were in Canada, he would seize her by the hand and drag her out into the street and catch a passing bus and just keep on going until they found a place to hide; but this was China, and in China there just wasn't any place to hide. "It's a lie, isn't it, Xiao Li?"

The girl looked directly at him. "No," she said. "It not lie."

"It's a lie."

The tears came into her eyes. "Mr. Sung help me, but I must be careful."

Derek knew what he had to say and he said it. "Xiao Li, I want to marry you." He pulled two letters from his pocket and handed them to her. "This is a letter from my mother and father giving me permission to marry you. And this is a letter from the Canadian Embassy stating my age and describing my family's position in society. Now, what you need is a letter from your mother and father. Can you get one?"

Her face brightened a little; she ignored Mr. Sung, who had suddenly looked at her. "Soon I go to parents in Daxiaoqiao. I talk them. You must come, Derek, you meet them too." Mr. Sung spoke sharply to Xiao Li, and she handed him the two letters Derek had given her; then she reached forward with her hand toward Derek. He took her hand. "You see, Mr. Sung say he read these. Also I must leave now. He try very hard to help, Derek. You must thank him."

"But when will we meet again?"

She opened her mouth to speak but someone was

talking loudly in a doorway and three men came out of it. They nodded to Derek, but their faces were impassive, and when they spoke to Xiao Li, they used quiet words. She looked quickly at Derek and, without a word, turned and walked toward the distant doorway, followed closely behind by the three men. Mr. Sung observed him for a moment and seemed as if he wanted to say something, but then he turned and followed the others.

Xiao Li's parents, Li Jianhua and Cui Maigong, lived deep in the mysterious *hutongs* of Ghengis Khan's ancient city. The great yellow brick walls of Xanadu had been torn down, exposing the buttocks of a city already ten miles by ten miles of narrow winding passageways and gates and court-yards, of small brick houses with dirt floors and whitewashed walls, without electricity and plumbing, and of ancient orna-ments broken by the centuries and the periodic political and cultural revolutions that invaded the narrow lanes with new policies from new dynasties. In Wangdao Lane you came to a gate crowned with a broken dragon head and turned into the courtyard littered with kettles and cooking ware, bi-cycles, a small vegetable garden, canework, and six door-ways to six small houses. The home of Li Jianhua and Cui Maigong was the one on the right, flanked on either side by large wooden barrels full of rare goldfish, one of which was called Poopoo, who was said to have descended from the fishtank of a silver polisher in the court of the Emperor Guang Xu. Inside the two-room house, the floor was con-crete, the walls whitewashed, the woodwork unpainted and crude, and across the bed, a Xinjiang grass mat; wires dangled like thin guts along the wall and ran between the small noisy clock and the hooded television set. The rooms had been swept, the house made dry and cool. The words of the political world were distant and unclear. Derek Usher sat upright in a chair sipping the hot Hangzhou tea, sometimes announcing a short Chinese sentence copied complete from his grammar book, and always when he spoke, the old people smiled at him but talked to one another as if they had just heard a panda speak the language of Man. Xiao Li sat to one side and between them with the body language of a stage director. The two old folks welcomed him to their home with a sly smile and squinted at him as if, though still a long way off, he had come dangerously close. They went and sat at a table of finely-chopped Mandarin delicacies and everyone began to relax a little and even to laugh. "They like you very much," she said. "They think you very rich, very powerful man. You like king to them." Derek considered the two old people and wondered why Chinese people, unlike Canadians, grew more beautiful with age. Xiao Li's father's face was strong and old as granite, the eyes hidden behind deep, puffy eyelids, seeing eyes, his shiny bald pate and wispy long white Buddhist chin whiskers making him look wise, and his mother, still beautiful in the eyes, the wrinkles creating a pattern of forbearance and wisdom. "My father say you strong man but walk like careful man. He say you speak good Chinese and must be excellent professor."

"Bu shi!" he said, protesting, *"Bu shi!"* Derek Usher sat looking at Xiao Li, trying to find his way back to the innocent face that had confronted him that morning many months ago on the sidewalks of Tian'anmen. It was a stronger face now, more self- possessed, convinced. There was a quiet desperation in it, a resolve, a knowledge that nothing could stop her. "You know," he said, without quite knowing why he said it at that moment, "what we are doing is very dangerous. It is a political act. Love is a political act. I am in love with you, and you, I think, are in love with me. That makes you a traitor and me a foreign devil."

Xiao Li's mother said something, and the girl caught her breath and looked into her lap for English words. "You are a *waiguoren,*" she said. "My mother say she not afraid of *waiguoren,* but many people afraid of *waiguoren.* Why, she say, you not find Canada girl to marry? Chinese girls do not marry *waiguoren.*"

"Tell her I am a friend of China. I believe in China. I live in another country, but I am a true comrade. I am sorry for everything that my people have done to China over the past hundred years. I come to pay for their sins."

Xiao Li talked to her mother for a long time, and when she finished, her mother looked as if someone had just tried to talk her into a magazine subscription. She spoke to Xiao Li in tones that sounded the depth of her confusion and disbelief. "This not enough," said Xiao Li, blushing. "My mother, she say if I leave her, if I go to Canada, she will have no person to look after her."

"Tell her we can earn much money in Canada and can send them more money than they can use."

Which she did. Cui Maigong seemed for the moment disoriented and poured more tea around the table.

"Tell her I come in the name and spirit of Bai qiu en dai fu."

Which she did, and Xiao Li's father, who had sat quietly for some time, finally erupted into speech, his eyes roving back and forth across the foreigner's face like beacons. At last she said, "My father say Dr. Bethune great Canada man who help China defeat Japan, but now China do not need Canada. Japan a friend of China. China now powerful country." Xiao Li grinned and blushed before she continued. "He say Xiao Li do not need *waiguo* for husband."

"Tell him," said the Canadian, "that now the *waiguo* needs Xiao Li for wife."

She smiled and a tear came into her eye. "No," she said, "it is impossible. I cannot speak these words my father."

"Tell him I love you."

She shook her head. "This kind of love," she said, "he know nothing about." Her father was talking to her, but she refused to listen. "He know love of this country."

"Tell him I love China." She studied him as if she had forgotten the words for it. "Tell him if you marry me, I will stay here with him." She shook her head again. "Tell him, I'll stay in China."

She translated his words and the old people stared at her for a long time, their hands silent in their laps. They refused to look at him. He had the feeling he was looking in past the boundaries of time into a world that had existed long before his own and would likely still be there a thousand years afterward.

5

The lights in the piazza before the Number Ten Dining Room have come on, the gas flame is orange and now hollow blue turning yellow, and you can still hear the tintinnabulation of the bicycles in the narrow lane that runs along the hotel wall, and high above the trees sails a silver slipper moon. Hagstrom grunts and rises from his chair and pads flat-footed to the kitchen, and returning with another quart of Beijing *pijiu*, pours himself a heady glass and goes back to the window to stare down at the giggling room stewards.

"So that's why he looks like a man who's written his own obituary," I say.

"What do you mean?" Hagstrom looks at me as if he suddenly discovers I'm there. "You know it took him two years before they gave him permission to marry her. A whole year of trains back and forth to Jinan and camping out on that bench just outside the gate of the shoe factory. Of course Sung took pity on him after a while and got the leaders of the factory to give him a room to sleep in. Even after Xiao Li's folks wrote the letter and spoke to the leaders at the *danwei* in Jinan, he wasn't allowed to talk to her unless he agreed to see her in a small room, where they sat on both sides of the table.

"He talked and talked and talked, and she took to remaining silent and staring at the floor. She knew all she had to do was refuse to see him. In fact she had on more than one occasion made up her mind to do it because of the pressure they had been applying to her. It wasn't like the old days, when they would make you wear funny hats and throw stones at you, but the pressures were there all the same. She was Chinese, she owed her responsibility to her parents and to the State. Only through patience, dedication and selfless devotion would China ever be able to hold up her head among the nations of the world, and if all the young educated ladies ran off and married foreigners, the country would surely return to the days of slavery and starvation. After all, the foreigner was only infatuated with her. He would take her to Canada and dump her. Everyone over there got divorced.

It was a country where drug-crazed teenagers broke into houses and murdered people sleeping in their beds, where motorists shot guns at each other from speeding automobiles and where people spent every waking moment of their empty lives filling their houses with electric gadgets, where material values took the place of social values, and where the state was run by people who got into office to pad their own wallets. Her children would probably grow up dope addicts and run wild in the streets and, in time, become unemployed and have to go on social welfare."

"You'd think," I measure out my cynicism, "if you had a billion people you had to feed 365 days a year, you wouldn't mind it if one or two of them went somewhere else to eat."

"You don't know anything about anything, do you, Ritter?"

"The more I know, the less I'm impressed."

Hagstrom rolls back and forth, the moon peering over his left shoulder, filling the room with a flat white light. "You see, in the West we hold human values very high, but we don't give a damn about people," he says, pontifical. "It allows us to move people around and do with them pretty much as we want, without someone always looking after us or watching us to make sure we're following orders. But here in China, people moving around makes everyone jumpy. Human values are secondary, even silly, compared to social and political values, but every fucking person is vital. Everyone. They can't tolerate one man's losing the faith. All it takes is one person, see? Maybe he makes too much money or maybe he sells visas or imports pornography, and the whole goddamned game is threatened."

"So just because Derek wanted to marry Xiao Li— ."

"They were all threatened. Everybody! Even after Derek and Xiao Li got permission to get married, they made her write a self-criticism and get up in front of all the workers at the shoe factory and read it to them, and at the end of her little talk, they got up and walked out of the room, and afterward no one would talk to her unless they could get her alone and tell her that everybody was behind her and they couldn't wait until she got away."

25

"So he's gone Chinese."

"Gone Chinese."

Hagstrom walks back to his chair and falls heavily into it and turns on the television set. It shows flags and flowers and a phalanx of high cadres standing on top of a concrete dam in Tianjin and making speeches about the wonders of technology. "You want to watch it?"

"I don't understand Chinese."

"You don't have to. Just look at the pictures." I watch for a while and then he says, "You don't mind if I go and practice my tuba, do you?"

I drain my glass and stand up. I'm a little fuzzy, and it isn't quite what I want to say. "That story about Derek and Xiao Li, you made it up, didn't you?"

He looks sheepish as he walks me to the door. "Would I lie to you?" he says, winking. "Derek's the one who told me the story, and I have rendered it unto you with all the eternal verities intact . . . rising action, crisis, falling action—"

"And a happy ending."

"Happy endings are important."

Below, on the sidewalk, I nod politely to the *fuwuyuan*, who sit on the bench and mark my passage with small smiles. The guttural simper of the tuba fills the ancient piazza with a melancholy mood.

PORGY AND BESS AND SUNG LI

Suddenly Sung says: "Listen to me. What I say, you must not tell anybody."

"I don't like this."

"It is necessary."

"I don't like that either."

Somewhere a telephone rings but nobody answers it.

"Okay, Del, now you must listen to me. I like study Western music. This is important. But you see, I can come study with you only because they give me permission. I must do something, you see. I must . . . tell them about you."

"Tell them what about me?"

"What you do, where you go."

I look up to the naked yellow bulb dangling from the crosspiece at the ceiling in my room at the hotel. "The rooms of the *waiguo* are bad places to talk about these things."

He drops his voice. "Don't worry, Del. This room is safe. I know. I know many things. And I know comrades in this hotel. I have spoken to them. They tell me be careful. They must be careful, too. Everyone must be careful. You must be careful. But never mind. I can come and go even if I have no pass. This is because of comrades in the hotel."

"Who are these people who want you to watch us?"

"There is only one man. He wants information. Most of them do not care about you. They care about me. They make sure about me, not about you."

"I wish you wouldn't have said anything."

"Yes, I imagine."

"Why are you telling me this?"

He leans still closer. "You know, I want you to help me."

27

I remember the night I met Sung. It was just another hot, stuffy summer night on the North China plain, a desert heat dry and full of lint dust but also sweetly scented with the thousands of square miles of vegetables that fed a billion people. The band was having some fun with 'Blue Bossa' in Independence Hall, the ballroom where once a month the U.S. Marines got everybody to dress up like it was 1955 forever and they owned the whole world and all you had to do was put on fancy clothes and do a little jitterbug or two and then things would never change. It was a long elegant room with chandeliers and flags and purple satin drapery and portraits of the Reagans. I went to open the windows and saw the young men sitting on the curbs of Xiushui Dong Jie, the street that ran from the Albanian to the Bulgarian embassies and captured somewhere in the middle, the American. Eight or nine of them, *liu-man*, toughs, and though it was dark, they wore mirror sunglasses and they brandished blue jeans and shirts with misspelled English words on their chests. They usually loitered around out there somewhere among the trees when the band got together and practiced. I had no idea who they were. I tried once talking to them, but the guard said something beneath his breath to them and they all wandered off, their tails between their legs. Now I watched them watching us, and the two Chinese soldiers stood at attention before the embassy gate watching me watching them watching us.

Jimmy Lanze had brought Sung Li to the rehearsal. Sung was a handsome man with one of those timeless Chinese faces you sometimes see chiselled into stones in the faces of Buddha— round, cave-like eyes, with mere slits, as if the eyes were hidden somewhere, like rattlers, and saw everything. He didn't need words to express what was on his mind. It was all in his face: it's been a long time, the face said, thirty-five years since liberation, thirty-five hard, lean years of great leaps forward and backward, realignment, corrections, fine-tuning campaigns against leftists and rightists, gangs of four and five and cultural revolutions and spiritual anti-pollution drives, but now it is the summer of 1985, now at last the millennium is at hand, thanks to Deng Xiaoping and the open door policies. You could see all that on Sung's face as he sat and watched the band working through 'Blue Bossa'. The face said, I know all about good changes and bad, I know some people think one of the bad changes is the legalization of dancing after the government opened the door to western culture just a crack and suddenly everyone in the country jumped up and started to dance; yes, they danced in the streets, they danced in dance halls, they even danced with their foreign friends at the hotels because the Chinese people are nuts about dancing, and for a while it seemed nobody could stop them. Still, everybody knew it had to be stopped somewhere. I knew, too, that in the spring of 1985 they outlawed public dances. Well, they didn't actually outlaw them; they regulated them. You had to have a certificate and a certificate required a good reason, and dancing ipso facto was not a good reason. The thing to do with the few foreign bands that were spawned during the liberalization was to neutralize them, bury them deep inside the bars and discos of the new steel and glass hotels where Chinese people normally cannot go unless they are businessmen or government cadres accompanying Western businessmen who will hopefully go back to Dallas and announce that they had been to Beijing and found it to be just like any other international city.

Copycat bands from Manila, which we called 'the music mafia', were hired to play all the hotel bars from Kunming to Beijing, from Shanghai to Xinghai. They performed Top 40 disco music cheerfully shorn of the ministrations of sex and violence, the ancient spider spirits of Daoist myth. So far as I knew, in the summer of 1985 we were the only authentic jazz band in the entire country. We called ourselves CHINA HANDS, a title we thought rather clever. We were a quartet and we played for the dances at the foreigners' waterholes: Jimmy Lanze on percussion, Gary Daw, who played alto saxophone in the style of Charlie Parker, David Lewis, a bassist who'd rather be out there playing rock-and-roll, and me. We were all right, good in fact. Lanze had played in clubs around L.A. in the early Sixties but now was a press officer at the embassy. He was the only one who spoke

Chinese fluently. Gary Daw studied at Berklee and claims he once jammed with Oscar Peterson and Ray Brown. David Lewis, well, he had never played with anyone, but in Beijing, where bassists come only one to a dynasty, he was much in demand. David was a reporter for Reuters and had been in China since 1978.

On the final chord of the tune, Jimmy introduced Sung to the band, and the Chinese musician took out an instrument that looked like a cross between a clarinet, a trumpet and an oboe, and, without saying a word, improvised wildly upon 'Blue Bossa' as if he had been playing it all his life. There was a lot of Gershwin in it, a snatch of a tune here and there from 'Porgy and Bess'.

So I say, "Help? How can I help you?"

"Will you help me, Del?"

"If I can."

"You see, my *danwei*, my work unit, is symphony orchestra. Next year we go on tour of America and Canada." He studies me closely. "You live in Kansas City in Missouri. You tell me this. You see, my orchestra next year play in Kansas City in Missouri."

"Great! Wonderful! I'll be there. You sure can count on me."

He looks for the right words, his eyes hidden in their deep caves. "Please listen," he says. "You see, I stay in America. I study modern music. I study disco. I study jazz. Yes, I study all modern music. And when I will return to China, I write modern Chinese music. You know, Debussy and Ravel and Gershwin, they study jazz to find a way to write classical music. China needs modern classical music. My country needs me. You see, we are very poor. We have only feudal music. Yuan and Ming music. This is good, but we have no true modern classical music since 1800— "

I have to stop him. "Wait a minute! Before you get carried away . . . tell me a little more about this spying business." He nods slowly. "Somebody told you to spy on us?"

"Okay, I come to your first dance at the Youyi,

remember? I talk to Jimmy Lanze that night. I make friend-ship with him. He speak very good Chinese. My English is not good."

"Your English is excellent."

"No, no. It is very bad. You see, I get permission from *danwei* to come to your first dance because I am professor in Central Conservatory and professional musician too and I write many modern pieces for orchestra. Of course they are very bad."

"So you were allowed to come to our dances providing you spied on us for your work unit."

"No, not my *danwei*. My *danwei* must ask permission from somebody else. Perhaps security people. A man come to my *danwei* and tell us it is not possible for Chinese people to play in foreigners' band. They are afraid I can be . . ."

"Contaminated."

"Yes, perhaps that. My father is good friend with somebody in the cultural ministry office and so I meet somebody who say he speak to security people and at last they say, Yes, you may play with foreigners, but you must also report everything you see. First, I say no, but my leaders, they come to me and say, If you do not go now, they think you are disloyal. You must go. So you see, I have no choice. There is nothing I can do. I cannot stay and I cannot go."

"But you came anyway. What have you told him?"

"Nothing."

"Isn't he suspicious?"

"No. Someone watch him too. In China everybody watch everybody. Everybody know what everybody else doing. Do not say anything. It will take time. It will take time. Maybe this is something you can never understand. You see, we are very old people. Too old. We are feudal people. We are also very close to one another. We think we must know all things about everything and at all times."

"So you're going to defect?"

"Defect?" He begins to laugh, but it turns to a frown. "Of course not. I am Chinese man. I can live in your country until I die, but I am Chinese man."

"So, you'll say you're just taking a short vacation."

"No," he laughs again. "That is impossible. I must

hide until they all go home. Then I must ask for political asylum."

"You will have to prove your life is in danger."

He withdraws his eyes and looks at the wall, looks through the wall at things I cannot see. "My life in danger already. I put myself into danger when I stay in your country. I am already refugee."

"You forget, Sung. Our countries are friends now. That means you don't mess with us and we don't mess with you. They call it friendship, but it's not really friendship. Not as you and I are friends." I can be cynical, too. "All it means is Americans are not going to support that little tinshop on Taiwan anymore. And if the Russians get heavy, the Americans will come down on your side. But it doesn't mean every Tom Dick and Harry or Wang Zhang and Sung Li is going to be able to hop on a plane and go off to study music for three or four years in the other guy's country just because he wants to."

"My friend, you do not understand China."

"Not from trying! I've lived here for three years now, but the more I learn, the less I understand. When I studied Chinese at Columbia, I knew everything about China, but when I arrived here in 1982 I was a little disappointed that China didn't measure up to my expectations. But I learned other things because I knew the language and I still could have written a book about everything. Today . . . I'd have trouble writing an article on China without contradicting myself."

"My dear friend, you do not understand China. You do not understand me. We embrace contradiction. Two things can be true at the same time. I should not come to the band, and I should come to the band. I should not be telling you this, but I should be telling you this. I should not go to America, but still I should. We are really a very simple people."

"All right, all right! You want me to help you."

"You must sponsor me. When I am in the United States, I call a man I know. He works in the Chinese Embassy in Washington. He talk to people in ministry in Beijing."

"I don't like any of this."

"Perhaps it is all right."

"Sung, what are you really going to do in Kansas City?"

"I study music."

"Sung, be honest with me."

"I am your friend."

"Please don't."

"Pardon me?"

"Please don't ask me to do it."

Sung joined CHINA HANDS one night in September in the Panda Room at the Black Swan Hotel, a tall concrete and glass slab in the northeast part of the city owned jointly by the tourist ministry and a Hongkong company. The glass tower was out of touch with the neighborhood *hutongs*, the puzzle-like ancient brick and mud suburbs that surrounded it. People rose early in the morning and walked around and around the hotel with the wonder of a small town awakened to find a spaceship had fallen on them during the night. At the Panda Room, a disneyish jungle of glass and bamboo, we played 'Round Midnight' and 'How High the Moon' and 'Yardbird Suite' and other classics, and just before the first intermission, Sung came up to the bandstand and played two lovely ancient songs on the suona, unaccompanied. The barroom went absolutely silent; the foreigners sat and listened and when he finished, they applauded feverishly and were joined by the Chinese bartenders and waitresses, who stopped what they were doing to pay him homage. We played next at the Beihai Hotel and the Xinhua Hotel before we decided to try something together. We took a minority song from Xinjiang called 'The Sunny Lake', a rather somber text, and let Sung play it through as written. Then he walked off the set as we jammed on it nice and slow, trying to preserve the mood and atmosphere but settling it down easy into the blues scale and improvising on the theme. We were just about to resolve everything into the final, closing chordal pattern when Sung stepped back onto the stage and began his own improvisation on the theme, and, after a couple of choruses before a silent house, we all jammed away at it until the end.

33

It would be an understatement to say that he brought the house down. The band applauded and the audience stood and shouted for more. It wasn't until later that Gary Daw remarked that it was strange the Chinese bartenders and waitresses, who had earlier applauded the Chinese song, had not joined the general celebration.

I was amazed at how easy the two music traditions had come together, or perhaps it would be more correct to say how easy we all played together, suona, saxophone and the rhythm section. It was as if we had been kidding ourselves with all our ideas about traditions and scales and temperaments, as if in fact we fully understood each other's music at the deepest level.

I asked him where he had learned to play like that. He said his uncle had brought a set of scores for 'Porgy and Bess" back from New York in the Forties. Sung's uncle had spent two years in Washington as a banker just before Liberation, and when he was ordered back to China because the Americans had backed the losing candidate, Chiang Kai-Shek, he slipped the scores past the customs people and hid them in a work shed during rightist campaigns of the late Fifties and then the Cultural Revolution. When he was a boy, Sung had memorized the entire score and could play it on every instrument he found. After the gig at the Xinhua Hotel, we began to learn more about each other's music. I taught him blues piano and he inducted me into the mysteries of ancient Chinese string instruments. It turned out also to be a language lesson because I taught him the blues in English and he taught the music of the Ming in Chinese. He showed me some of his own compositions and without thinking, of course, I insisted that the band play some of them at the hotel bars of Beijing. At the same time, with much flourish and ceremony, I was invited to give a performance of modern music at his *danwei*, followed by a lecture on Western harmony. Then one night late in the Spring of 1986 in a concert at the Fine Arts Institute, Sung Li took my place at the piano and played a piece he had just written called 'Night in Tianjin', a tune structured over the changes of Dizzy Gillespie's bop anthem 'Night in Tunisia', which employed a whole tone scale, and, on the last chorus, I sat beside him on the bench and we played the hell out of the bebop riffs over the top of the bass and drums.

After the show one of the leaders of the school came up on stage and shook everyone's hand but Sung's, and later, on our way to the car, I saw the two of them in an alleyway deep in conversation. I asked Sung about it on the way back to the embassy, but he only smiled at me. One week later we played at Maxim's, a large, elegant French nightclub, but Sung failed to show up and when I saw him the next time, he told me his leaders had spoken to him about his performance at the Art Institute and made him stay home the night of the gig at Maxim's and compose a long self-criticism.

They said it had been indiscreet of him to get too close to the band, and that he ought to perform ancient Chinese music with a Chinese rhythm section. They thought he was going too fast. They said he was too quick to adopt Western ways. They said they heard that he had argued that China should get rid of some of the leaders at the top because they were too old. They heard too that he had once argued that musicians should not eat out of the big iron rice bowl, but, instead, live off the proceeds from the music they write. They wanted progress, too, but they wanted slow, controlled progress. They argued that music was too important. As important as rice. It should not be squandered. It must express serious purpose and ideals, it should lift and direct the masses, it should release the energies of China toward production and national principles. It should not be 'yellow' music.

"The Blues is yellow?" I asked.

He explained that 'yellow music' was anything new and fun, anything that expressed a bourgeois point of view. He had no choice in the matter. He could play for dancing, but it must be refined and logical. He could play for listening, but it must not inflame ugly thoughts. He had written one hundred pages of self-criticism and read it out loud to them, and then they took the composition along with them for further study. He had to wait for them to approve it, and if it was not strong enough, then he would have to write it again and again until he got it 'right'.

One night I invited Sung to my hotel. We went to the

hotel roof-garden, where African students drank and tried to make out with women of any color or creed drifting in from the language institutes, and where Japanese secretaries sat and plotted ways of avoiding marriage with their Japanese bosses, and where foreign experts from every country in the world sat together and pretended it was still possible for the peoples of the world to get along with one another. Sung seemed uncomfortable sitting among the international set and when he went to the toilet, I saw someone talking to him. They talked for some time. When Sung returned, he refused to answer my questions about it. I knew something had gone wrong. Perhaps his comrade network had broken down. He was angry when I tried to pursue the matter. He got up and walked out. There was something stubborn and proud about him, some quality of character I couldn't figure out at that moment: something like an inner strength and resilience, a toughness that I would never know, an instinct for survival, a strength of will in the face of insult. And when later I walked him to the gate— he had to be out of the hotel by ten o'clock— and said goodbye, I watched him walk out into the night and move along the street like a man who knew exactly where he was going and what to do when he got there.

"But you are my friend, Del."
    "If I am your friend, you won't ask me to do it."
    "You are my friend. I must ask you. I would not ask you if you are not my friend."
    "Ah, there we are different. Very different."
    "What do you mean?"
    "You are my friend. I would never ask you to break the law for me."
    He seems perplexed. "You are speaking words I do not understand."
    "You paid the price before. What price are they asking this time?"

Now it's after nine but still the heat's oppressive. Sung and I have gone swimming at the International Club and enjoyed

a quiet, leisurely meal of Guangdongcai— Cantonese food—
and because it's hot in the streets and because we've laughed
too much and consumed too much wine, we take a cab out
to my hotel without thinking much about what we should or
should not do at that time of the night. We pass in through
the hotel gate even before we know it. Cabs are never stopped
at the hotel main gate. They just wheel in and out, the guards
occupied with bicyclists or pedestrians. It is generally as-
sumed that only foreigners had enough money to ride in cabs,
but if, for one reason or another a Chinese person rides along
in one, he probably has a good reason for it. Our cab takes us
around the quiet, dimly-lit oval drive and stops before my
apartment building and lets us out, and we walk clinging
together and singing an old Hui ballad beneath a peach-hued
moon to a doorway covered by a reed bead curtain to keep the
flies out. A *fuwuyuan* nods away at his desk in his little
cubicle just to the left of the door, and when he sees Sung he
asks him for his pass. But since Sung has not checked in, he
has no pass, and so the night clerk tells him to check out at
the main gate. But without a pass, he cannot check out again.
Catch-22. He also cannot arrange for a cab to take him back
out through the gate because the cabs are strictly for
foreigners. What I could do is go back out to the gate and hire
a cab, come back to the apartment and pick up Sung, drive
out, around the block, and, on our way through the gate, stop
and allow Sung to go into the office and fill out a request for
a pass . . . the very absurdity of it makes us both laugh until
the tears roll from our eyes. But wait, there's a simpler way
to do it! All Sung has to do is stay the night with me and then
in the morning he can ride out with me in the car that comes
to take me to the Banking Institute, where I teach Western
business methods to students who had never laid an eye on
a personal cheque in their lives. Nobody would ask any
questions of a Chinese riding out in a school car early in the
morning. But a Chinese spending the night in a foreigner's
room with or without the knowledge of every Chinese author-
ity in the hotel was an act of treason.

But in this case, this clerk knows all about Sung, and,
thus, has to ask him to go back out to the gate. They get into
an argument. Sung turns and, with his head, directs me up-

stairs to wait for him.

I walk to my pocket refrigerator in my cubbyhole kitchen, fetch a quart bottle of *pijiu* to the sitting room and set it unopened on the small round glass table. In time Sung comes and sits before me without a word, and I watch him glowing darkly in the dull yellow lightbulb of my coffin-shaped room. He's internalized. He looks out of place, even in his own country. He looks like a man who's just been deleted. The sheen is gone, the frolic in the eyes vanished, the skin papery dry. Poor Sung, always to live like this. A stranger in his own land. But then, that's why he's my brother. That's what I recognize in him. I forget he's Chinese and he forgets I'm a *waiguo*. He knows how I feel because that's how he feels. I haven't even had to put his thoughts into words for him. He knows without my telling him that I have given away the best years of my life and surrendered a promising career in a quiet, wealthy college in Missouri and at the summit of my career— some people actually said that if I trimmed my wicks for another ten years, I would likely become the first Black president of the college— to spend three years in China in a vain attempt to teach banktellers the facts of life, myself all the while living a half life behind walls within walls and eating cabbage and leeks laced with MSG and salt, observed and feared, and although I have tried to teach without preaching capitalism or socialism or populism or even communism, which is something I have long been attracted to, and have also tried to live without complaining about the food and the suspicions and the supervision, I have often felt betrayed by the long, awkward ceremonies and empty rhetoric of my official Chinese "friends" and "col-leagues" and even angered by their refusal to accept me as a plain, ordinary human being.

Living in China is something akin to being in a 747 that has lost all its engines somewhere over the Rockies, and in its long wild descent into Seattle, you sit and listen to the crew's calm instructions, which you just know to be pure propaganda, and you cling to the idea that you're riding in a time-honored and safe machine, and you oscillate and twist feverishly between hope and despair and you begin to pray for an opportunity never again to question your own silly little daily routines.

Suddenly Sung says: "Listen to me. What I say, you must not tell anybody."

"I don't like this."

"It is necessary."

"I don't like that either." Somewhere a telephone rings but nobody answers it.

"What do you mean by price? What is price? You are my friend."

"Sung, you paid the price to play in the band by spying on us. What's the price for being allowed to study in America?"

"I do not work for secret police. I am not spy. In America, I never hurt you, my friend. Do you think I ask my friend to take me to his country and let me sleep in his house and make friends with his friends and drink his wine and then spy on him and his country?"

"You say you have a friend at the Chinese Embassy in Washington."

Chinese people do not touch each other much and they never touch foreigners. Especially Black foreigners. Never. But at that moment, Sung reaches out and lays his warm hand across my arm. "When I not return to the Motherland, I lose my Party membership. I lose my citizenship. They write me and say I never be able come home again. My father and mother are disgraced. They lose rice and oil coupons. They must continue live in the old house in hutong with cockroaches and bad sewers and now their son has become traitor, their neighbors stay from them."

"Is it worth it, Sung? Is it really worth all that? You know, one thing I have always respected about the Chinese people. They put other things— people, the soil, the country— before themselves."

"Yes! It is worth while. You see, I must write great Chinese music. This is my duty and my honor. I must take big chance. And one day my country thank me. They invite me to return and they perform my music." Suddenly there are tears in his eyes. "You must tell no one what I say. You must be very careful now. You must forget what I say to you now. You must wait for me in Kansas City."

"You would dishonor your own mother and father?"

"My father a proud man. You do not know my father. You see, he is famous man. He kill many Japanese invaders. Chairman Mao honors him. In my house is big certificate signed by Chairman Mao. So my father tell me I must do this thing. He say he is old now. My mother is old now. They are poor. They live in old hutong near the Old Palace. He love the old days. He love the new. My father say that I must be hero. It is very strange. I must leave my Motherland to help her."

"Contradiction."

"Yes," humorlessly, "contradiction."

"Sung, what makes you think you will ever return? In America you can be famous. You can be rich. You can write music without the government ripping up the score."

"This is my home," he says quietly, now composed. "These are my people. I cannot harm them. Del, you cannot understand these things. You do not have feelings like these. You have told me so. Yes, I know you fight for many things. You believe in many things. But you do not understand how we depend on each other. We are like one part of one whole. I am refugee in the world if I stay out from the Motherland. These are things you cannot understand."

"You are wrong, Sung. I understand. In some foolish way maybe I even envy you."

Sung rises slowly and moves toward the door. "I must go now," he says. "The *fuwuyuan* has been very polite. I must go back to the gate now. Please, let me go alone. I talk to them. Some of them are comrades." He smiles and shakes my hand as if I have just met him for the first time. "Don't worry. Everything is fine. I call your room tomorrow."

"*Zaijian*, Sung."

"*Zaijian*."

I watch him as he moves beneath the bright, blossoming crabapple trees and out toward the lighted street, but tonight his walk is tentative.

THE NEW BETHUNE

1

A yellowing, wrinkled portrait of Chairman Mao smiled down upon George Hendrix.

The room was cold and the wonky cracked windows were stuffed with old yellow newspapers to keep out the Mongolian seep. Across the slate-grey dragonback roofs of the city, the ancient drum and bell towers stood upright pale and defiant shadows. The shroud of industrial pollution made it all seem alien. It was a city without a soul. Economics was not enough, he thought, consumerism and sound fiscal policies and balanced reserves, these were not enough. These people had once believed in something! In drum and bell towers, for example. In golden temples and palaces and monkey kings and mass marches and war and in children tossing roses at soldiers.

That was why the Chairman was smiling down at him: he had given the people something to believe in. What had gone wrong? They had come and smashed down the golden temples and belled the monkey kings and driven prophets and professors and other heretics around town in gravel trucks so that the people could throw stones at them and shout slogans and put them into closets for ten years and let them out only to clean latrines . . .

George Hendrix got up slowly and went to the broken window. The glass was stained and dark, and he had to lean close to see anything. He took off his glasses and leaned still closer, and even as he did so, there was a rattle at his door.

"*Qing jin!*" he barked, awakened.

It was Professor Hong. "I see I am disturbing you," he said. "You are busy."

"No, no!" said George Hendrix, turning, wiping away a tear. "No, I'm waiting for a student."

Professor Hong looked down the hallway for the elusive student. He was a small round man who wore small round issue spectacles that made him look even smaller and more round, and though he had taken to Western suits and ties while men his age and station clung patriotically to old, faded blue Mao uniforms, he nonetheless walked about with an air of caution. He peered around corners as if at any moment he thought he might be dragged out into the street and put into a gravel truck and made to wear a tall funny hat with slogans on it while his students threw stones at him.

"Don't your students keep appointments?"

It was a loaded question. "Not lately, they don't," Hendrix said, loading the answer.

Professor Hong balanced there in his suit and tie. "It is your students I want to talk to you about," he said, nervously. "Do you mind coming 'round to my office for a short chat?"

Professor Hong had mastered the English language but he wasn't quite sure what to do with it. For now, at least, he was content to enlist it in the struggle to bring some order to an institution so hopelessly feudal that it would require a fleet of gravel trucks to haul out the deadwood and still there would be something left of inefficiency and feudalism. Professor Hong was a modern man. A scientific man. He knew down to his socks that it didn't matter what colour the cat was so long as he fetched in the mice. But Hong was more than modern. He had been educated at Edinburgh, he had heard enough to think twice about things. Hendrix had got him to agree, for example, that human beings possessed 'souls', but he had argued that they were not, in his humble estimation, 'pus bags' that you hauled about with you in a 'fallen' world. Hendrix pushed him along in hopes he would set out his thoughts on the matter, but Hong declined. He was, after all, a survivor of all sorts of treacheries both foreign and domestic.

42

Hendrix followed him out into the hallway. An old charwoman had just gone the length of it with a wet mop and laid a thin coat of ice which would have withstood the frantic onslaught of the Montreal Canadiens. She stood at the far end leaning over the handle of her mop, obviously pleased with her work and amused that she had made it difficult for the two old professors to get about.

Hendrix skated into Hong's office. In China, rank hath no privilege: the office of the chairman was just as cold and dark as his own. "Please," said Professor Hong, pointing to a chair, "do sit." Hendrix sat and crossed his knees to show he was not intimidated by sitting before a standing administrator. Hong appeared to be considering his words for some time. "As you know," he said at last, "we . . . that is, the young teachers in the department, have not had the benefit of hearing native speakers, and since some will be going abroad next year to study I thought perhaps it would be— "

"You're going to ask me to teach another class, Professor Hong, and I'm going to have to decline. We've spoken before about work loads."

"Not another class, professor."

"I already teach fourteen hours. Back home we call it 'the exploitation of labour'. I think it was Marx who used the phrase. But then, you know more about Marx than I do."

"No, not another class. You see, well, the students of Class Three will be going out next week on a work project."

Hendrix uncrossed his legs and sat up. "In the dead of winter!" He tried to tame his voice; it was necessary to remain calm in these circumstances. "Surely, you can't be asking them to go out into the countryside and dig irrigation canals in the dead of winter."

"No, no!" laughed Hong, embarrassed. "Nothing quite so bad, nothing so bad."

"An ice rink then?"

The two of them looked for words to a conversation that appeared to have gone off the track. Professor Hong stood on one foot and then the other, and Hendrix retired to his locked-knee position. It seemed then that the native speaker would have to be the one to untie the Gordian Knot, and Hendrix knew there was only one way to do it. In the sanctity of the office and alone, he would let God speak for him.

"It's because of what happened, isn't it?"

Professor Hong stared at him. "I'm sorry?"

"You're taking my class away from me."

"I'm afraid . . . I don't understand, Professor Hendrix."

Hendrix uncrooked the knee. "It was Sui. Xiao Sui," he said, more to himself. "He told you about it. He came to your office and told you about . . . the . . . well, look, I was only trying to show them. Sui, he never understands a word I'm saying." Hendrix paused for a moment and fixed his eyes upon the man standing over him. "There's only one reason for his being in the class anyway. I suppose he had to do it, but you know, you never asked me why I did what I did. You know, I am a *waiguoren*, I am a foreign devil." Professor Hong tried to laugh. "He wouldn't understand. Ask the other students in the class. Ask them!"

Professor Hong smiled down on George Hendrix, who refused to smile back. "I'm afraid I do not understand— "

"Of course you understand, Professor Hong! You understand perfectly!" Now he had done it. He had let his temper get the best of him. Hendrix looked at his watch and, like Houdini, unlocked himself and sprang to his feet. "I must get to my bus. It leaves in two minutes. We can talk about this another time."

"By all means," said Professor Hong, disturbed.

Hendrix declined to be polite. He turned away without smiling or saying another word and strode to the door, threw it open and stepped into the hallway. His feet scooted out from under him and he flew sideways for a while and then sprawled onto the ice.

Grammar he knew to be one of the more noble human endeavors. It enabled the least articulate of men to lay out thoughts in an order perceptible to others. The right words in the right places, saith Hemingway . . . and Hendrix might have added, and in the right tense, number and mood. Grammar he knew was also one of the best and brightest ways to convey the Very Word of God.

Anyway, he hadn't been nearly so successful with sociology. He had gone into sociology with the best of intentions, but somewhere along the line he had been distracted by science and synthetic economics and social systems which merely perpetuated the myth of materialism. He had had a strict moral upbringing and a loving but brutal father against whom he had often laboured in vain; in fact, the more he laboured against him, the less he succeeded, and in the end had merely thrown himself onto the mercy of being middle-aged. He struggled for some time in a university managed by bookkeepers and communists who spent most of their creative energy sleeping with each others' wives. In the 1960s Hendrix got interested in the riots of his students. It was, suddenly, a world of sensual adventurism and political action. He divorced his wife and ran off with one of his graduate students, and together they walked picket lines and sat on train tracks to stop the troops from going off to Vietnam. And when the university got its chance, it denied him tenure, and he was sent out into the cold streets to look for work. He knew only one thing: teaching. He fell to his knees, and his young wife ran off with a younger, more politically-aware man. He began to drink and smoke, he went to expensive group-gropes in Oregon and California.

It had to end somewhere.

Thus immersed one hot afternoon in the warm blue waters of a Los Angeles swimming pool and grappling with a naked woman half his age just to prove the five-hundred bucks he had invested in the workshop was well-spent— yes, he could hold a meaningful discussion with a naked woman without having to reach out and stroke her legs— suddenly, brilliantly, perceptibly he saw God. Just above the trees there. Over a little to the west. Right there. Yes, right there, in a pink cloud He was, reclining, muscular, pastel, with a giant fist and with one finger crooked out toward him . . .

The naked woman in his arms said, "Do you want to sleep with me?"

. . . beckoning . . .

"Excuse me, but do you want to come back to my room with me?"

He looked at her. "No," he said, slithering away toward the cool blue edge of the pool. "No, I have to go now."

"What?"

"I have to go. I have been called."

"What are you talking about?"

Hendrix pointed with one hand toward the sky. "He has called me."

The girl turned, then, to look to where he was pointing and thought he was talking about the life-guard.

Well, maybe it wasn't quite so romantic as that. After all, he had to tell that story so many times that somehow it lost all its clarity. But what remained was that hollow sick feeling he had in the pit of his belly, that awful recognition that he was being possessed, packed off, driven away and under instructions.

Hendrix 'had grown up in Pontiac, Michigan. He received his education in the cellar of the Grace Christian Methodist Church, where Mrs. Lettie Hammer— the smallest and sweetest soul in the whole town— had idly informed him one Sunday morning that he was the proud possessor of an immortal and imperishable soul. She smiled down at him beatifically and pronounced him one of the Chosen Few who had come into the world endowed with some special kind of radar that allowed him to locate the Absolute Truth, though it lay hidden in a pile of dung. She told him there was no way out. He was damned with a commission: he was going up to Heaven whether he wanted to or not. God Himself was up there somewhere, and little Georgy was down here. God Himself was up there somewhere, lying on a cloud and trailing his finger through the stream of glory that bathed all human existence, just above the trees, watching little Georgy and waiting for him.

"You'll have to be very, very careful, little Georgy," she had said, smiling, "because you'll never know when you will be called."

It never occurred to him it might be that very moment when the beautiful blond nurse from Ventura swam toward him, her little brown nest flashing at him from below the water like a seam of gold. But it was his destiny to swim away from her, to escape from the snake-infested waters and go forth to seek the God of Clouds.

He walked that afternoon, and walked. He fell several times because he had his eyes fixed upon heaven. At last he came to the Pacific. Now it was dark, dark, dark, and when he kneeled in the sand and studied the yellow light far away in the west, he realized something had just died in him and something else had come. A spiritual erection. He got to his feet, took off all his clothes and walked out into the water. It was hard to say what happened after that. All he can remember is being rushed off into the city inside a howling ambulance. He went to Saskatchewan and got a job teaching in a missionary school on a reserve, and after that went out to Lagos to work with refugees, which, in turn, took him to Hongkong, where he worked as a counsellor in a camp run by the Holy Light World Service. He knew he had at last arrived at the very place toward which his life had been leading.

Now it was God's move.

John M. Rowe had come down from China to talk to the counsellors about the opportunities among the People of the Dragon. It was, he said, time to reclaim the People of the Dragon for God the Father Almighty, Maker of Heaven and Earth. He told them about the university system and about the foreign experts living in a huge hotel in Beijing and about how these people had been selected to teach English in order to bring about the modernization of the country. He spoke of the obtuseness of the bureaucrats, of how easy it was to bring God into the classroom and the country back to His Church. Hendrix didn't appreciate all the duplicity and crudeness, but he admired Rowe's zeal, and most of all he dreamed about the huge, over-ripe plum just ready to be plucked. Yes, it was ready to be plucked. Yes, it was time for missionary work. China was a military dictatorship that denied God. Marxism was materialism at its worst. It was high risk. The stakes, on the other hand, were high.

The communists denied the existence of God, said Rowe, and spoke of Him as the chief opium peddler in the Orient, and even while they allowed a few churches to reopen their doors, they also made lists of those who entered therein. Communism, he said, bowed and kowtowed to the idols of secularism and confiscated property and civil rights and reduced people to the lowest common denominator. Worse, they viewed the human being as a mere compound of dirt and animal charm which, under the right conditions, could be re-fashioned into an order only slightly higher than the ants.

Communism was the Anti-Christ.

Hendrix thought about China. Even as a boy, his mother had warned him not to dig too deep in the sandbox because he might fall through the hole and come out in China. China was down there somewhere, he figured: all he had to do was dig for it. Food was another thing. His mother always said, Think of all the starving children in China. He didn't like spinach. Think of all the starving children in China. They could have his spinach. Yes, indeed, it was all part of destiny. He was fated. One day, after all the wars and famine and flood and chaos and godlessness and over-population and revolution . . . It was all in the cards. There was literally nothing he could do about it.

They'll call you 'foreign devil', said Rowe. They'll vilify you and crucify you. Sticks and stones. George Hendrix knew he was an intellectual, he had a proper education. His own society had exorcised him. It was all part of the plan. He couldn't help any of it. Now he stood at the gates of China. It had come to that. China needed him, needed his expertise. He spoke English, and apparently China would sell its soul for it. Very well, he would buy it.

So simple, so very simple.

Most things are. Norman Bethune, for instance. Bethune had come out to China during the Japanese War and brought along with him the very skills for which his own nation had exorcised him, and the Chinese worshipped him and established him in the national pantheon, right up there alongside the Chairman and Zhou Enlai. God the Father, God the Son, God the Medicine Man. Bethune had had a messianic vision of medicine, and Hendrix had a messianic vision of grammar. What was the difference? Bethune had said, Lend me your poor, your huddled and wounded soldiers and I will bind up their bodies. Hendrix would say, Lend me your poor, disillusioned college students and I will bind up their sentences and restore them to The Moral Universe.

It was the right time, and he was the right man.

2

The girls all sat on one side of the room, the boys on the other. And it was cold. They stared at him from beneath their heavy blue layered clothing as if he were some sort of statue with the gift for speech. Few of them took notes on what he said, either because it was just too cold in the room or because they simply didn't know how or because once they got into the institute, there was no way to get them out again until at last the government found something for them to do.

He took his reading book and stepped down from his podium and stood in front of the ranks of girls. "Wish for something, Xiao Chen," he said. "Anything . . . just make a wish." Chen Jun was beautiful, intelligent, the most promising and thoughtful student in class. She had revealed too much to him in an essay. She had described her grandmother and confessed to her having once during The Great Proletarian Cultural Revolution hidden a Christian Bible in a bag of rice. The old woman had often read the Bible late at night in her room, and Xiao Chen had sat and listened to her. When she died, Xiao Chen made certain that the Bible went down with her into the grave dug crudely alongside the train tracks of Hubei. "Wish anything, anything!" Xiao Chen had come on two separate occasions to his room at the hotel, once when he and the other experts were holding a prayer meeting. She and Ding Ling and Wang Mingchu. The three of them had expressed a desire to learn more about Christianity after

49

Hendrix had worked his way through a short essay by Bertrand Russell, the heretic.

"I wish . . ." said Xiao Chen. "I wish the Motherland were more rich and more powerful."

"I wish . . ." he repeated. "I wish the Motherland were rich. Subjunctive. Does anyone know when we use the subjunctive mood?" He looked around the room. "Xiao Ding?"

Ding Ling sat up, frightened. "The subjunctive indicates something . . . contrary to fact. You must imagine this or hope for it."

"Very good, Xiao Ding. Put Xiao Chen's sentence back into the indicative."

She thought for a moment. "The Motherland is rich and powerful."

"That's a fact," said Professor Hendrix, looking quickly to the very back row, where Sui Li sat. Sui Li was the class monitor and the one who relayed everything said in class back to the Party Leader. "Is it a fact? Is China rich and powerful? Yes, but Xiao Chen wishes she were more rich and more powerful." Sui was a tall handsome lad with thick jetblack hair and a Mongolian slant to his forehead, a contemptuousness, distance on the features of his face, as if he believed firmly that he sat in the very centre of the world. Sui Li had once translated for the Party Leader at a banquet and Hendrix noted that while he was busy trying to sort out everything he was saying, the Party Leader was eating up all the sea cucumber in oyster sauce. "China is rich and powerful now, but Xiao Chen wishes she were still more rich and powerful, and so we can say, 'If only China were still more rich and powerful, we would be happy.' Do you understand?"

Some stared at him coldly. He would have to try again. It was time for him to make his move.

"Okay. 'The world turns to God and the world is saved.' Turn that into the subjunctive, Chen Jun."

Chen Jun looked at him for a moment. "If the world turned to God, it would be saved."

"Right!" he said. He said the sentence several times, and then he made each of them repeat it, but when the sentence reached Sui Li, it ran up against a rock.

"Sui Li?" said Professor Hendrix, when the student refused to speak. "If the world turned to God—"

"I do not believe it," he said, baldly.

Hendrix blanched. "We are discussing grammar, not belief."

"We do not believe God."

Hendrix glanced about the room. "That is not important," he said, slowly.

"What do you mean," said Xiao Sui, "about 'turning'? How do you turn?"

"By prayer," said Hendrix. He had not slept well. It was the MSG in the food, it was cold in the room, his ministry had turned to sand. "We Christians believe in prayer. It is a form of communication. We ask God to help us make the world a better place. I help China become richer and more strong with the help of God. I pray to God to help me."

He had said too much. He went back to his podium and hid behind it. He looked down at them. They seemed to him to be parishioners in pews. They waited for him. "Prayer is the way a Christian speaks to God. There is no simple way to do it."

"Show us," said Xiao Sui.

Hendrix preferred to be less direct. He liked teaching God through grammar, through sentences dressed and disguised. "The voice must come from within, through silence. Reverence. The Christian bows his head and folds his hands together."

"Show us how," said Sui. "Is this the way?" Sui placed his hands across his nose and nodded several times with his eyes wide open. The class laughed at him. Hendrix knew they were embarrassed. It was the kind of laughter he had once heard at Hangzhou when a PLA soldier had waved a handful of smoking joss sticks and planted them in sand before an altar. "Is this correct?"

"No," said Hendrix. "That is Buddhist."

He showed them how Christians pray: he dropped his head and folded his hands together in an attitude of total concentration. There was a flicker of nervous laughter in the cold room. Hendrix looked up in time to see Xiao Sui smirking.

"Will you pray?" he said. "What do you say?"

Hendrix stared at him. "Are you so interested in all this, Xiao Sui? Are you really interested?"

"We are all interested."

The class was quiet now. All he could hear was the growl of trucks going down the narrow, winding road past the institute.

"All right," he said, smiling. "Everyone must fold their hands together . . . like this." He watched them copy his movement. "Now lower your head in an attitude of prayer and close your eyes . . . and repeat after me . . ." They dropped their heads and he dropped his. "Our Father," he began, "Which Art in Heaven . . ."

The words ran out between his lips like escaped prisoners and he felt as if each one sped through the sunlight of Shakespearean orotundity that was his blessing from above. And, as he spoke, he felt himself leaving his body and flying about the room, circling, circling. When he finished with an operatic Amen, he lifted up his head and opened his eyes. They no longer sat there as a congregation of suppli-cants, head down, hands folded in respect, but, rather, forward, eyes thrust open like a hot little audience at a strip-tease, and he looked down quickly to see whether he had forgotten to zip up his fly.

And Xiao Sui was nowhere to be seen.

3

Hendrix lived in a hotel.

Well, it wasn't actually a hotel. It was a ghetto for foreigners, a fur-lined ghetto. The Russians had built it for themselves in the early 1950s because there wasn't anything in town good enough for them. Unfortunately, they weren't around long enough to appreciate it. The Chinese threw them out. They were, of course, communists too, but they weren't *that* communist. Hendrix's rooms were dark and Dos-toyevskian, with antique and noisy plumbing, high ceilings, bare wires, dark wood, gloomy windows, cockroaches. He lay in bed all day and contemplated his lot. Luckily, nothing had been broken. God had saved him. They had run several machines over him at the Shoudu hospital and found him fundamentally healthy. It never dawned on him till the third week, however, that they were keeping him in bed and in his own rooms because they didn't want him skating around the ice rink hallways of the institute.

The old nurse from the hotel clinic told him that he was 'not good in head' and gave him some pills that tasted like perfumed mud. She told him to stay in bed until 'head good again'. He felt a little weightlessness from time to time as he struggled across the room to his toilet or to a chair in the sitting room, where he watched television. Nothing was interesting on the television. Still he sat and watched old men in Mao coats wagging their fingers at a country that learned their lessons in computers, agronomy and grammar from them. At night he tried to figure out what was happening during the endless domestic tragedies and grand operas but often went to sleep sitting there. If he sat too long in his bath, he found it difficult getting up again. Once he slipped climbing into bed and fell to his knees, and it felt as if someone had come up behind him and hit him over the head with a shovel.

He told Trish Marley that it was all because of the class monitor. "I know he went straight to the Party Leader and squealed on me. He couldn't even wait. He set me up and then left the room even before I was finished."

"I think you've been hurt," said Trish. She was in the fellowship, a woman of forty-five winters, a woman who dyed her hair and worried about her figure only a little less than she worried about abortion clinics and the world-wide communist conspiracy. "You ought to lay back and relax."

"It didn't just happen, you know. It was all planned."

"I think you scrambled some eggs up there."

"Nonsense. I'm fine."

"Your marbles done rolled."

"I've got to get out of here."

"You want to come with me and be my love?"

"Trish, get me out of here."

"They'll send you home in a box if you don't take it easy."

"Don't worry about me. I'm getting out of here on my own."

"Are you kidding? There isn't one good hiding place in this whole country."

"Go."

"Where?"

"Leave me alone."

"I'll say a prayer for you."

"You do that."

She was right, of course: in China every stone was numbered and every *tongzhi*, every comrade, knew the numbers of the stones and how to arrive at each stone when he was supposed to, so that, presumably, at any moment on any given day somebody somewhere knew where everyone else was and what he was doing. It is said that China doesn't need any secret police— though of course it has a large and efficient force— because every person watches every other person all the time.

All this was doubly true for foreigners. It wasn't only their high visibility, it was also the number of stones to which foreigners could go. The city was surrounded by signposts that said, No Foreigners Beyond This Point. Anywhere a foreigner went, he towed an impressive crowd along with him.

George Hendrix pondered all this, and it made his head hurt. Anyway, he thought, there are really only two places I can go— home again or back out to the institute as fast as I can so that I can get a crack at the young teachers. It wasn't time to quit. He had to make sure he had access to the Chinese. It didn't matter whom. He didn't care whether Professor Hong was attending his classes and writing down everything he said. He was going to give it a run for its money. Nobody could say he was a quitter. He liked a problem, he liked a challenge. He was always ready to accept defeat, but he felt he had to earn it first. He had to fail. His life had been one long line of failures, but he had risen above it because he knew it was only a test. God was testing him. He dropped his head and had a long discussion with Him about his current plight.

He had tunneled down through his sandbox, through topsoil and bedrock, through cisterns and pools, fire and molten sand and back out again to just exactly where his mother had warned him against. China. Now he'd have to find his way around his newfound land. He'd have to wrestle the buggers to the ground. He couldn't run for the corner every time they threw a punch at him. So he left at six-thirty in the morning. The *fuwuyuan* were all still in their beds, so he wouldn't be snared in their early-warning systems. He saw only an occasional jogger. It was damn cold. There was a patch of ice here and there—jaws and maws. The guard at the gate had tired eyes and sore feet. Hendrix seemed more an object of movement than one of the foreign devils to be watched. He walked north to the intersection, where he could catch a bus to the institute. At that time of the morning Beijing was just like any other city in the world—long, empty boulevards and winking traffic lights, bird-calls from the winter trees, one lone truck lumbering through the concrete canyon like a visitor from another planet.

He went to the bus-stop, a cement platform with a corrugated plastic roof. He sat down. He was tired! Dizzy, sick to his stomach. He ought to go back and try again tomorrow.

Two people came and observed him silently. He felt the menace of the cold coming up through his feet when the bus came. The three of them climbed aboard the packed bus, and a nice young boy gave Professor Hendrix his seat.

"*Xie xie!*" he said, patting the boy on the head and smiling at his mother. She smiled back at him and then looked out the window.

It was fifteen minutes to eight when he reached the gate of the institute, and he could scarcely catch his breath. He stepped over the log wired to the gateposts so that bicyclists would have to dismount and be examined by the old men who kept "the bad elements" away from the school. Hendrix looked up at them. There were four of them, and they sat drinking hot tea and gazing down at him like huge, painted devarajas guarding ancient Buddhist shrines. Hendrix smiled and waved to them and hurried to the main classroom building. He knew exactly where he was going, and he knew how to get there.

The home-room of English Three was on the second floor and just across from the toilets, which stank. The students called them 'the beard of the dragon', but he would have preferred to call them something closer to the hindquarters. He clung to the wall to catch his breath. A few young people skated around in the dark hallways, and he followed them up the steps and along the cold concrete corridor. The lights were out. He had a headache now. He wasn't sure where he was. Usually the hall was illuminated by high, tiny, yellow 40-watt bulbs that only declared the up and down of things, never their extent.

He wandered along the corridor until he smelled the breath of the dragon, and he knew he was home.

A distant white outside light reached toward him with frigid fingers. He put his ear to the door. Silence. He was too late. They had gone off somewhere. They had another teacher, another room.

He tapped at the door and entered without waiting for an answer. Xiao Wang was sitting at his desk and reading an old copy of *China Daily*, Xiao Jiang was asleep, and Xiao Chen, bless her! stood at the window looking at the horizon.

"Good morning, class!" he said, breathlessly. He walked to the teacher's desk, stepped upon the wood platform, and held on tight to the podium. "It is cold today. The frost is on the pumpkin." It was the formula he used every day, and as he said it, he pulled his books from his bag.

Xiao Jiang's head popped up and he rubbed his eyes as if he saw a ghost. Wang tried to smile as he rolled up the newspaper. Only Chen. Dear Chen! She stood there, her back to the window now, the white light falling across her shoulders, and her face bore a mixture of relief and surprise and, even, horror.

"Xiao Chen," he said, "I wish you would take your seat. Subjunctive mood. It indicates wish or preference . . . contrary to fact, since at this moment you are, unfortunately, still standing."

She ignored him, looking for words.

"Where is everyone?" he said. "Don't tell me they're out somewhere digging holes in the ground. Intellectuals should never do that. Their purpose is to lead . . . to show the workers and the peasants the way."

"They will come," said Jiang.

"Future," said Professor Hendrix.

"Teacher say you fall," said Xiao Wang. "You in hospital now."

"I am returned from the dead," he said, laughing. "Passive Voice. "The object becomes the subject of the sentence."

The door opened and three students walked into the room.

"Good morning, Xiao Gui, Xiao Ni and Xiao Huang!"

It was as if someone had slapped them across their faces— they stopped and stood there until Chen said something to them in Chinese, and they went to their desks and sat down. Chen walked to the front of the teacher's desk and looked up at him.

"Now, can we get on with this morning's lesson, Xiao Chen?"

Chen said, "You are not in hospital? They say you are in hospital and cannot return."

"As you can see with your own eyes . . . introductory clause, followed by a comma, and here's the main clause. I am NOT in hospital. As Deng Xiaoping saith, Trust your own eyes. I am in the classroom. Indicative. It indicates fact. Reality. Truth. Why don't you just take your seat now so we can get on with the class?"

Xiao Chen stood her ground. "Professor," she said, quietly, her eyes lowered, "I am sorry to say, Professor Hong is now our teacher."

"Professor Hong!" he said.

"Yes sir."

"Since when?"

"Since you go to hospital," said Xiao Wang.

"Went, Xiao Wang," he said, angrily. "Since I WENT to

hospital. Past tense! But as you can see, I did not go to hospital. Now, Chen, please . . ."

She was about to say something when the door spun open. There were three more students in it, talking gaily, and behind them, round and smiling, Professor Hong. When they saw him at the desk, they stopped and stared.

"Professor Hendrix!" said Professor Hong. He came and stood beside the platform, trying very hard to smile. "What a surprise! What a surprise!"

"Yes," said the man behind the desk, prayerfully, "yes, I imagine. I imagine it's quite a surprise." He smiled, adding, "Imperative mood."

FORBIDDEN CITY

1

Sudden the motions, stiff, unpredictable, and when at last he came, he came to destroy her as if her body were a sanctuary long denied. There was always pain, always violation, riot, a kind of looting, and then, just as quickly as it began, it ended and he retreated into his darknesses. It was hard to say whether she enjoyed it. Say she allowed it to happen, say it happened, say it was going to happen whether she wanted it or not.

She lay for some time listening to him sleep and then got up and walked out of the bedroom to a long narrow sitting room and across the room to a window looking out upon a courtyard of blossoming and breathing apple trees. In this place she was a stranger, though perhaps not so much as the man in her bed, who had been born here. A forbidden city this, yet it had not always been so. The first time— it was the late 1970s— she had been a *tongzhi*, a comrade, and they had loved her because she had left her comfortable life behind and journeyed thousands of miles to struggle on behalf of the masses of men and women who had thrown off the shackles of the Gang of Four.

So long ago!

She smiled at the moon. It was a white ghost drifting among the courtyard trees and filling them with eternal light. Never had she seen such a moon over Kamloops, where moons always steered a high, otherworldly course. She looked for words to describe the quality of the luminescence, but no words came. She thought of the way the painters made moonlight into a creature of *this* world and the poets printed their picture poems vertically to the paintings. What did the poets say? She had always wanted to "see" what they said, but she had had to depend upon Xiao Li for that. He seemed thrilled to know she did not know. "Come on!" she'd say. "What does the poem say?" He'd only smile. "What's that supposed to mean?" And he'd say, "I know what it say but I cannot tell." Language was Xiao Li's refuge. He often ran away from her into Chinese, using words she did not know or playing hide-and-seek by misusing English or providing a nonsensical translation, and she'd have to go in after him, using her 'chinglish'.

Anyway, Xiao Li hated the moon. Just before they got married— they already had a letter from the Canadian Embassy— she brought him to the hotel and took him into the gardens before the theatre and sat him down on a bench to look at the moon. "I hate it!" he'd say. "I hate the moon!" He could get more ice into his words than anyone she had ever met. "Moon always look down at you!" She tried to hold him, to calm and console him, tried to remind him it was only a matter of time and she could take him to Canada and then he could get what he always wanted to get, learn what he wanted to learn, yes . . . he could be a *man* in Canada. In those days he loved the idea of Canada; it was something like China was to her. Ideal, exotic. They were reaching blindly toward each other's worlds, perfecting that which each held to be imperfect in his own.

"Xiao Li," she said, "don't hate the moon. We think the moon is the symbol of love. See, it always comes out at night . . . to help lovers find each other in the dark."

"I know where you are," he said. "*They* can see. I do not wish *them* to see." Xiao Li lived in a world that made everyone's business everyone else's business. "*They* must not see."

"Why not? We not doing anything dirty."

"Dirty?"

Always Xiao Li's English teacher, she said, "Dirty

means you shouldn't be doing . . . well, what you're doing."

"We do nothing dirty."

"No? In my country we couldn't be doing what we're doing?"

He was silent because he didn't understand. "I not dirty."

"Look, Xiao Li, I am your teacher . . . that is, I used to be your teacher, and you were my student. That's a no-no where I come from."

"No no?"

She leaned into him. "You have a lot to learn about us, you know."

"No chance to learn here. No reason. No future, no hope. So poor, so many people. What is use?"

His words hurt. "I can't wait to get you home," she said, taking one of his hands. "We'll get you into the college and you'll learn English and then you can go on to medical school . . . the sky's the limit, Xiao Li!"

"Limit?" he said.

Xiao Li was a child of the Cultural Revolution, and she was a child of the Age of Aquarius, which made them equal in that they had both yet to pay the dues of the Sixties. Xiao Li was a child at the time, but she was already married and pregnant. Still, she carried high the banners and occupied the campus and smoked pot and denounced the war while her husband stood on the sidelines demanding that she "act her age". Once they took her down to the police station and booked her for "obstructing traffic", and when she came out, she carried her baby daughter to the photographers and made a speech about a green, peaceful world. Right after that, her husband left and got a court order to take the child with him, and so she went back to college and tried to become a teacher.

She had often asked Xiao Li about the time the Chairman came down off Tian'anmen and posed with Xiao Li's group of Young Pioneers for the foreign press photographers, but he never answered her, always stared at her as if he couldn't understand what she was talking about. She knew it had happened because his mother had shown her a picture of him— a small black-and-white snapshot she had hidden under the floorboards when the Red Guards came to her house looking for foreign and old things to burn out in the road.

"I am no student now," said Xiao Li. "I am worker. I am street-cleaner now."

"Not for long," she said. "Soon I shall whisk you away on my magic carpet!"

Of course it was not quite so simple. The little man at the desk said, "Teacher Elizabeth, this letter for you. Our leaders say now you must go back to Canada." He showed her the memorandum. "Xiao Li must now return to his unit."

"I am afraid we have a contradiction," she said. "You see, I have here in my purse not only the permit, but also the letter from Xiao Li's work unit and from his parents and my university and my parents."

He tried to smile but it was so cold in the office, he seemed trapped in his flesh. "The permit," he said, "is no longer valid. You will understand."

"Then I shall apply for another one."

"I am afraid that is impossible."

In those days she knew what to say and how to say it because they knew she was working for them and she knew if she practiced restraint, if she refused to quit, if she merely sat in her chair and refused to leave, if she refused to get mad, then in time they would have to do what she wanted them to do.

"Lao Ruan," she said, quietly, "in a few months I shall have to begin packing to go home. There is a lot of paperwork, a lot of packing, a lot of forms, there is a lot of money you have to pay me . . . it would be better for you and better for me if we could settle this matter and I could get back to my work."

"But we have . . ." He stopped, looking for words.

"*Guiding*," she supplied. "You have *guiding*, I have *guiding*." She held up her expired permit, the letter from Xiao Li's work unit, the letter from the Canadian ambassador. "I shall buy Xiao Li's ticket and all expenses . . . but I need soon to begin because of all the paperwork."

The first time she came, she stayed at the hotel and often walked among the trees in the courtyard and imagined herself in some sort of ancient temple plotting conspiracy against some wicked emperor. She imagined herself dressed in fine silks and fitted with a phoenix crown, followed by faithful retainers. She walked with long, confident strides, she had nothing to fear from the shadows cast by the pale moon. Now, it was merely the middle of the night and she had been violated and abandoned. Xiao Li had taken out all his frustrations upon her, had visited and ruined her, had relieved himself, used her, and afterward abandoned her.

But what else could she do?

She was forty-two, she had burned the bridges, torn up the roads. She had been away from Kamloops too long, they had forgotten her. Even her magazines no longer came. She was a woman without a country, too odd, too set in her ways, an old hippie, an NDP Waffle, remembered only because of the picture of the long-haired and braceleted woman holding up a baby with her arms still cuff-linked and surrounded by 'pigs'. "Stop the testing," she had said. "Make the world safe for my baby!" She had learned the hard way that the Sixties were over, the Seventies still-born, and the Eighties a time to hide in her office and try not to make a noise so it wouldn't give them a good reason to lay her off.

When she got Xiao Li back to Kamloops, they saw how young he was, how good-looking— a read stud! Carrie Ladd had said— and they had laughed about it behind her back because, of course, they knew she had taken advantage of the beautiful young student in a country where, perhaps, such kidnapping was still possible. What they didn't like was how she carried him about like a red banner, making all conversations turn about the subject of New China.

They were not surprised when they stopped going out to parties because some of them saw Xiao Li but rarely and then only at the Chinese restaurant on the lower edge of town, and often drunk too. Betty Warner spoke to her about it, and she told Betty Warner to mind her own business. It seemed, however, that they all knew something was going wrong, and yet she proceeded with her own teaching as if everyone ought to mind their own business. So he was a young stud! They were jealous of her, bunch of bitches! Spent their whole life studying to be teachers and then discovering nobody wanted them anymore, and that, in the end, the only thing they had was their classes, most of which had at least one or two studs in them . . . but the righteous bitches seemed able to overpower their own deep needs and urges and avoid 'contact' with students and studs. It wasn't only that. It was their naïveté. They knew nothing of the world around them, drew sustenance only from material gains, political innocence.

Only once did anyone come close. Clell James, he was an historian, widower, too old to be a threat to anyone. He told her, "He doesn't seem such a bad boy."

"He's not," she said, punctuating it with her fist on the table. "He's not a bad boy."

"What . . . seems the problem? Is it just a matter of settling in? Is that it?"

She gazed out into the haze above the city as if she saw Xiao Li's face in it. This was a question she had often asked herself, and since she had received no answer, merely shrugged her shoulders. "It's going to take time," she said. "These things take time."

"Yes," he said, thoughtfully. "Right now, I imagine it's just a little culture shock. He probably thinks he made a mistake leaving China."

"No," she said, "he hated China."

But she knew she was lying to herself: Xiao Li did not hate China at all. He wasn't so sure about Canada.

A deep trench angled across the courtyard. It was a deep, a bloody wound, it was always like that. They always interfered with Nature, they always came in the Spring and dug ditches and then filled them up again, but they always left a scar. If any part of the hotel was in flower and in peace, they came

64

and dug it up and piled dirt everywhere. It was because they were 'fecal', they were anal, they wanted to smear their feces across the wall and then write their names in it, and their slogans, always their slogans. This was something she could never understand, it was something that made her forever a stranger here. No matter how long she lived here, she would always be the outsider, the *waiguoren*, the guest. Even the Europeans and the Americans who had come here in the 1930s and 1940s, they were still 'guests', they would never be accepted as anything else, ever. This was a fact. It was a fact in a land of facts, and it was a fact, too, that Xiao Li could never escape, even if he tried, and, of course, he had tried, and failed.

At first she had reached out for him and he had reached out for her, but now they each knew that somehow, somewhere, they had been betrayed.

2

The Voice of America fell into their little room like acid rain. The words were hard, small and sharp, and she spun the dial looking for the BBC but kept coming upon Radio Moscow, another storm front full of yet another kind of fallout. Finally, she turned the radio off and went back to Xiao Li, who sat at the small round table with a glass cover over a pale blue and embroidered table cloth. He was drinking black coffee and stirring a small bowl of smelly rice gruel with tiny salt pickles in it. They had never taken to each other's breakfasts, though Xiao Li picked up a coffee habit in the restaurant in Kamloops. She never had anything but a cup of coffee, though occasionally she ventured into the small, sweet puffy morning bread called *youtiao* which Xiao Li fetched back from Renmin Daxue, the university just north of the hotel.

"What are you going to do today, Xiao Li?" she said. She hadn't wanted to say it; in fact, once it was out of her mouth, she began to examine her own motives and found that she was very, very tired from having spent the night watching the moonlight.

He glanced at her before sampling his warm gruel, and said, "I go to parent . . . take to Friendship Store this day."

Xiao Li used only two tones when speaking English: approval and disapproval. When he approved, he sang out the words and polished them, like apples, but when he disapproved, he clipped each word to a sentence as it if were an item of laundry pounded white and clean.

"Do you need money?"

"No!"

She had stumbled, now she fell. "I owe you fifty *kuai*," she said, quickly, "I took it out of your wallet to pay for the tickets to Datong."

"I do not need money!"

She looked away. It was morning, and a beautiful morning at that. In spring the weather in Beijing was so damned unpredictable: one moment it was blustery and Mongolian, and the next, light and airy, mystical. After deforestation, the government had undertaken a massive greening program, but still the air was full of fine grit and the skin often felt like sandpaper. She spent most of her time applying lotions to her fragile body in an effort to stop the flaking.

She knew she had to recover something in him, and so she flicked her eyes back at him and reached across the table, laid a hand across his, said, "I'm just trying to do the best I can . . . under the circumstances, but don't you know how hard it is?"

He looked away.

Like a teacher, she reached for his chin and took it, rolled the head about and drilled her eyes into his. "What you are doing, Xiao Li, is perfectly understandable, and you must see that what I am doing is also perfectly understandable." But his eyes were blank. "We *are* going back to Kamloops, there is nothing you can do, there is nothing I can do."

As usual, his face was a mask, a beautiful, a tragic mask, a Peking Opera mask. Xiao Li was a character in Peking Opera, a tragic prince, an injured Everyman, and she, she was a minor courtesan, one whom the emperor preferred to the first courtesan.

"I *can* do something!" he said.

"What?"

He breathed in deeply and took up the small antique knife he had been polishing, flicked it open and examined it quietly. He had half a trunk full of antique knives, some from the Ming and Yuan dynasties, valuable if not lethal. Most of the knives frightened her, but he took such delight in restoring them, polishing, sharpening them, making small labels for them, reading about them in old books. They came in many fantastic shapes and were richly ornamented, in brass and gold. One had a smudge on it which Xiao Li claimed to be blood.

"What?" he said. He flicked the knife open and ran his finger along the blade, testing it.

"What can you do?"

"I can . . . stay."

"Where?"

"In my home."

"You do not have permission to stay in your own home. You are a landed immigrant of Canada now. You are no longer a citizen of China."

"I can go to . . . Language Institute."

"You do not have permission to study at the Language Institute."

He flicked his eyes at her. "I can stay with Xiao Ruyu, her home."

"You do not have permission to stay at Xiao Ruyu's home."

It was, however, Xiao Ruyu that she feared most. "I have told my work unit," she said, "that we are going home right at the end of the school year."

He looked trapped and turned the knife so that it was pointed at his stomach.

The first time she saw Xiao Ruyu was out on the street just south of the hotel. The government had planted cotton-wood trees and lilac bushes, laid walks and flower beds and benches. At night the benches were full of young lovers, whose faces were merely touched by the high yellow lights

67

above the boulevard. She had waited for Xiao Li in the apartment until after nine and then gone looking for him, expecting to find him at the corner with his pals, drinking beer he purchased with his vaunted *waihui*, what little he had left after he traded most of it on the black market for the despised *renminbi*, the People's Money. He usually got double for the *waihui* and spent the profit on the knives. She searched the store and went out into the dark again, past the bus-stop thronged with people waiting for buses already crammed to the gunwales with other people. She walked on the path between the low painted iron fences and then she saw his bicycle. She paused, thinking it had been stolen or perhaps forgotten. She studied the license plate and was about to leave when she saw two people sitting at a bench beneath the trees, its back to the street, and on the bench a man and a woman, lovers, her head inclined to his shoulder. She knew the head, it was Xiao Li's head, but surely it was fastened to someone else. Someone had stolen his bicycle, and his head.

She spun about, her breath coming only with great difficulty, and shé was halfway down the block before she recovered. She knew she was feverish, her hands tingled, she was short of breath, and people were staring at her. She turned, then, gathered herself and went back to the bicycle.

"Xiao Li!" she called.

He stood up quickly, turned. It was so like Xiao Li. It had to be him. It was his face. His stoney face. The mask, the silence. He said nothing, too. That was his sign. Suddenly, she felt foolish, confused, and, instead of running from the storm, walked straight into it like one who had lost her wits.

"This is Xiao Ruyu," he said, but she scarcely heard. She was watching him, drawn from his depths, yet wishing to drown. "This," he said, looking at her, "is my wife, Elizabeth."

"*Ni hao*," said the girl, plainly.

She said nothing, turned and walked back under the lamps and along the street and into the hotel and along the dark and dangerous paths of the grounds and up the stairs and into her room. It wasn't until she was home that she was able to think about matters. And later, when he returned, locking the door behind him, coming into the room, she said, "What is your relationship with this girl?"

"Relationship?"

"Who is she?"

He slumped into a chair and observed her darkly. "Xiao Ruyu," he said.

"Who is Xiao Ruyu?"

It was always like this, hunting down guerrillas in the weeds of his own language.

"Cousin," he said.

"How? Your cousin?"

"Her uncle is my uncle, too."

She laughed. "Kissin' cousins!"

He didn't understand. "Xiao Ruyu's mother know my mother."

"How convenient!"

"We children together. Same street."

"Why didn't you introduce her to me before we got married?"

"You ask . . . many questions, Li zi!" When she came too close to him he used her Chinese name. It was necessary under these conditions to keep calm.

"Not once did you mention her name before we got married."

"No!"

She spaced her words as if speaking special English, enunciating consonants and giving full value to vowels. "You two seem very close," she said. "You were childhood sweethearts, I gather. Her family is close to your family." She moved closer and sharpened her teeth on her words. "You have not told me that you have been—"

"It not correct!" he said, as if he was taking part in a struggle session in which he would now move into the second part, namely, self-criticism. "I know it not correct! I did not tell!"

She wanted to make him kneel before her and hold his hand up in the air behind him. They called it "jetplane" during the Cultural Revolution; Xiao Li had seen it done many times. She wanted to place a tall white dunce hat on his head and write in Large Characters, "I Am An Adulterer!" She wanted to put him on the flatbed of a truck and parade him around the hotel so that they could throw stones at him and call him names. Instead, she got to her feet, balled up her fists and shouted, "You double-crossing bastard, you!" and fled to her bedroom, slamming the door behind her. She knew she had lost him. It was all over now. She cried, she let him hear her cry.

Yes, she was a stranger here. She was a stranger in this country and she was a stranger in this marriage. She was a mere 'guest', a *waiguo*, just as in Kamloops Xiao Li was a 'Chinese' or, worse, a hyphenated Canadian. Almost but not quite.

3

The college squatted on a hill over Kamloops, and every morning at seven-thirty, Xiao Li clambered up over the dry benchland past the rattlers and sat in classes, and every afternoon at five he slithered back down again and went into his room to sit and stare at words that stood distant like stars in an immovable black jar. He worked long and hard but accomplished little. At the end of the first term he discovered he had failed three of four classes. His teachers told him that he was bright and industrious but lacked the words to manifest his intelligence and that he'd never get anywhere at the college on the hill until he learned to speak the language.

So he enrolled in a night class that met twice a week. English at ground zero. Time weighed heavily on his hands. He got a part-time job scrubbing the big transcontinental rigs that pulled into a gas station cafe, a menial job which somehow he learned to enjoy. He made friends with a gang of boys from Hongkong and went with them for late night visits to a Chinese restaurant in the Thompson River bottomland, often returning home a little tipsy and, she soon discovered, horny. One morning at six he came back by taxicab. She sat at the breakfast table watching him stumble up the walk, hair dishevelled, shirt-tail out, a bandage around his head. He had a long story and told half of it in English and half in Chinese, but none of it made sense to her. In time she got the full story from Xiao Li's English teacher, who had heard it from the other students in class. The night had begun innocently enough: a ride to the restaurant, some high-jinks, noodles and beer, wild talk carried on in Chinglish (Xiao Li of course spoke Mandarin, the others Cantonese, and English proved to be a leaky raft), and then somebody began to talk about politics, a subject none of them had the least interest in, having been force-fed such matters since childhood, stuffed with slogans and axioms and rhetoric till it turned sour in their brains. Strangely, however, they began to talk like their fathers and for a while began to think they believed what they were talking about. One of them said if it wasn't for people like Xiao Li, they'd all be in Hongkong making money and getting girls, and Xiao Li laughed out loud and said if it wasn't for the other guys' parents and grandfathers who had fucked up the whole of China in the Thirties and Forties, they'd all have stayed home instead of sitting around in a stupid restaurant in a stupid city speaking a stupid language.

Ordinarily, they would have let it go at that. Maybe it was the liquor. Words got hard and meanings soft, and nobody got so much hurt by them as humiliated, and then someone (it was never discovered who) threw a punch at Xiao Li, and Xiao Li punched back, followed by a general melee; and the restaurant owner called the police, and the police came and hauled them down to the station and booked them on disturbing the peace and fighting in a public place and told them to come back the next day to tell it to the judge.

She went to court with him and heard the judge dismiss the charges with a warning.

Xiao Li went home and locked himself in his room for two days. When he came out, he told her he would have to quit school and his job. Yes, he had lost face. He wouldn't go back out to the college and see the boys from Hongkong, and because one of the kid's uncles worked at the highway

71

garage, he'd have to quit his job there, too. She left him to himself for awhile. She didn't want to be his mother. He had to learn to survive on his own.

Instead, he hid in front of the television set, where, coming home from school each night, she'd find him sprawled, half-asleep.

"Did you go down to Hudson's Bay today?" she'd say, having poured herself a stiff gin tonic. He wouldn't even look at her. "I told Bob Fitts you'd give him a call today about that opening in the stock room. Remember?"

Xiao Li shifted his eyes and stared at her as if she were a television screen. "What is stock room?" he asked.

"Well, where they keep stock. Naturally. Where they ship things . . . or maybe they receive them. Inventory, that sort of thing. Interesting work."

His eyes went hard as if to indicate he considered such work vulgar.

"Why, Xiao Li! You have to start somewhere."

"Start! Start what?"

"What are you going to do all your life? Sit around watching television?"

He went back to watching television as if he intended to go on watching it all his life.

"What are you watching?"

"Nothing."

She tried to watch it with him. After a while she got up, feeling a little giddy from her drink. Xiao Li needed help, and she knew where to find it.

She called Dan Goodenough at Manpower the following morning, and Dan told her about the new employment counselling workshop they were starting out at the Reserve. She drove Xiao Li to the class the very first night and saw eight or nine Indians, a couple of wild young girls from town, and, sitting behind a table as if she were frightened of her own odours, the counsellor from Vancouver. She let Xiao Li drive her car to the classes after that, but about a week later, she got a telephone call from Cache Creek. Xiao Li told her he had wrapped her car around a tree, and would she come and get him. She took a friend's car and drove for two hours through the canyon, only to find Xiao Li and the two girls from the Manpower class sitting in the police station. They had found a lump of hashish as big as the Ritz in one of the girl's handbags. Xiao Li refused to talk about it all the way back to Kamloops, and she got so angry at him that she pulled off the road and began to cry, but he sat there way over on his side of the seat staring straight ahead as if he could see the television set all the way from there.

She bought a new car, and Xiao Li began to collect welfare payments.

Every Tuesday morning he dressed up in a suit and walked down to the welfare office, where he stood in line and gave the fat lady his name, spelled it out for her several times, then wrote it out himself, while everyone in the room sat and stared at him, and then he sat and waited for his appointment with Ms. Jenkinson, who came out her office door and shouted his name so loud you could hear it all the way to the street. And when he got to his feet, they all looked at him again, and he tried to smile at them. Ms. Jenkinson was from Ottawa, her father had been a public servant, but she had married a railroad man and come out to the Interior to live. She had but one true love in her life and it had nothing to do with social work. Often, during her interview with Xiao Li, she asked him whether he had yet found Jesus Christ. She told him that prayer produces miracles and upbraided him because he had not accepted her invitation to attend the Saturday Night Gospel Sings at her church. Ms. Jenkinson knew that if for one night she could get her hands on him, why she could march him right up in front of Pastor Daegle and that would be the end of him. Often, during her interview, she would drop her voice and ask him whether he would like to get down right now on one knee, and she'd say a prayer for him, but he refused because he was frightened to death of her and because she sounded like the Red Guard who had once come upon him looking at a book in English one of his friends had pulled from a burning pile.

He went home and told her that he wasn't going to go pick up any more welfare cheques, and then she heard all about Ms. Jenkinson.

73

She planned to go down to the Welfare Office herself and register an official complaint about Ms. Jenkinson, but, instead, she let the claim lapse. Xiao Li spent the remaining days in his room, friendless, unemployed, penurious, dependent on her. There seemed nothing to do about it. She couldn't get him a job, she couldn't teach him English, she couldn't send him home again, and, in the end, she couldn't even interest him in going to bed with her unless she got him good and drunk first, in which case often he would spring out of his dark mood and lay siege to her, which made her black and blue for days afterward.

Then a miracle happened.

He met Lucas Sempler. They called Sempler "Cool Hand Luke" because he was a Mountie and because he had a collection of antique guns in his basement. Xiao Li met him at the Holiday Inn, where he had taken a part-time job parking cars. Luke used to hang around the garage, and the two of them struck up a relationship because one of Luke's grandfathers had been a doctor in a missionary hospital in Jinan, China. Soon, the pair of them would go up into the hills on a "shoot", and Luke told her that Xiao Li had a good eye. One day he gave the boy a shot-gun, and then two, and soon, Xiao Li began to collect guns, too. In September, he decided not to go back to school, but, instead, to go out shooting with Cool Hand Luke.

But Luke himself, it seems, got badly injured one night in a high-speed chase through the Fraser Canyon, when a semi rig ran him into the ditch. He was taken to a hospital in Vancouver and transferred to a local detachment there.

Holiday Inn installed an automatic parking lot in November, and so Xiao Li was once more without a job. After that, his only outings were to the dry hills above the city, where he went with his guns to kill rattlers. Once he shot a big one and brought it home, skinned it and tried to cook it, but it tasted foul, and they had to throw it out. It stank up the whole house for a week afterward.

4

The marriage permit was renewed of course, and they filled out more forms and sat in cold empty rooms for interviews and lectures, and at last, they signed the cards and watched while the petty official imprinted his red seal of approval.

They went out and took a public bus back to the hotel and registered with the *waiban* as man and wife, filled out more forms so that Xiao Li could obtain a new set of identification cards—work card, residence card, purchase card, bicycle card, hotel card.

"I am new man!" he smiled.

"I am a new woman!" she laughed.

The *fuwuyuan* in her doorway must already have been told that she was marrying a Chinese man because they were all there in their little cubbyholes waiting to see them walk up the stairs and lock the door behind them. She tried to be gracious about it, but she could tell from their eyes that he was an object of derision and envy. He was, indeed, no longer one of them, but he was not yet a *huaqiao* either, an overseas Chinese. For the moment they could get at him. Everywhere he went, he had to put up with their eyes, their slurred voices. No matter what they said, it always came out the same way. "Eh, Comrade!" they'd say. "You got one, eh? You got one of them to hang onto so's you can run away, eh? Soon you'll be free of all this, eh? Well, not yet, eh? You've got to get your boiled water until then, and someone's got to clean your room and bring you your laundry." She did her best to neutralize the difficulties by interacting with the *fu* herself. But they seemed always to be everywhere, in her rooms and out, everywhere. His adjustment was slow. In fact, he learned how to avoid the *fuwuyuan* by staying in the rooms and having her bring him food from the dining room, and when she took him in a taxi to the Friendship Store, he took to wearing dark glasses and sport shirts so that they might think him from Hongkong. She couldn't, of course, know exactly what he was going through because she wasn't going through it herself and he couldn't tell her because he didn't have the words. He made friends with one of the *fuwuyuan*, and she often caught the two of them in close conversation; he seemed to be confiding something he hadn't been able or willing to confide in her.

Xiao Li's family came to stay with them at the hotel. The mother stayed for a month while the father was in the hospital so that she and Xiao Li could visit the sick man and feed and care for him, and then the father came for a month to recuperate; Xiao Li's sister came with her child, Little Sky, and stayed for a couple months for no apparent reason whatsoever. She said nothing because she knew it was the custom; in fact, she gave them money and bought them a television set and refrigerator. Often Xiao Li stayed, as well, with his family, and she went along, but she early on learned how to avoid doing so because Xiao Li's sister lived on the eighth floor of an apartment which had only a part-time elevator but a full-time staff who went around making everyone's movements public information.

"She say she come to Canada," laughed Xiao Li, one night after his sister walked downstairs. "We send her money, she come to Canada."

"Sure," she said, "now come on, it's been six weeks since we've been alone. Let's go to bed."

He lay there, his hands to his sides, his feet pointed straight down, as if he were going to be buried. She touched him and he felt like granite, she kissed him and elicited only the slightest response, undressed and slid up against him and untied his pants. She had to fight him, and he fought back, with stiff, controlled movements as if he was being lectured by a voice deep inside, instructing him in the proper and correct motions, but in time he listened to no voices as he struck out at her and tried to break off all her limbs.

5

The Russians had built the hotel they lived in. It was a dark, secretive place, with long, narrow, coffin-shaped rooms laid out everywhere with the same severe orthodoxy, and all the apartments were given a narrow, dark hallway that joined the kitchen, bath and sitting room. It was in this hallway that the old chest stood, and in the chest was Xiao Li's dagger collection. He had spent most of his energy and innovative skill on building drawers and levels inside the chest and gluing liners everywhere and affixing small, carefully-written labels to the drawers. The chest itself was a Qing master-piece, with deeply-carved figures on it representing the Eight Immortals Sailing Across the Seas— an obscure legend which even after she had it explained she found inscrutable. It had a beautiful, etched brass latch on it, and a brass nail pushed through it to lock it. Often when she returned from her college, she found him bent over the chest and fondling the daggers, speaking quietly to himself. It was as if, somehow, he were communing with some voice deep inside the chest which only he could hear.

So it was, that afternoon, she found him huddled over the collection, speaking, but the voice came not from the chest but from a person sitting in the next room.

It was Xiao Ruyu.

"*Ni hao,*" she said, rising, smiling coyly. She was very pretty, small, delicate, with ruddy cheeks and an outdoor hardiness.

"*Ni hao.*"

They worked small phrases on each other, and Xiao Li explained that Xiao Ruyu had brought a newspaper from her father. She suggested that the girl stay for supper, but that was out of the question, the girl had to leave at once. Still, she thought, this was the first time Xiao Ruyu had ventured into the inner sanctum of their lives. After the girl left, she took Xiao Li to the dining hall, where they found a corner table by themselves. The food was warmish, whitish, slightly tasty, and twice the price she would have had to pay for it back in Kamloops. Not only was she no longer a *tongzhi,* she was being ripped off by the hotel at prices which were constantly referred to as 'readjustment' but were in fact galloping inflation.

"Have you told her?" she said.

"Her?"

"Xiao Ruyu." He said nothing. "You must tell her that soon we will go back home."

"Home," he said, laughed quietly to himself. They ate quietly for a while, but then he stopped as if he had broken a tooth off on a stone in his rice. "I have no home now, Li zi."

"That's silly."

"No. I have no home now."

"You have two homes. Canada and China."

"No."

They were surrounded by noisy, happy people. It was no place for their conversation.

"Xiao Li, you've got to stop kidding yourself. You have the best of both worlds. You will soon have a Canadian passport, and with it, you can come and go as you see fit." He didn't seem impressed. "You can sell your dagger collection. You told me once that the Yuan dagger alone was worth $20,000! It takes me a whole year at the college to make that kind of money."

"Don't sell daggers."

"Why not?"

"I give to Xiao Ruyu."

"Oh, that's going too far, Xiao Li."

"They say daggers stay in China."

"They?"

"Guiding."

"What *guiding?*"

"New *guiding.*"

"Okay," she said, resolutely, "with or without the daggers, we go."

He said nothing.

They rose and paid the bill, and on their way back to their rooms, he walked sullenly behind her, his hands deep into his pockets. She waited for him and then tried to steer him to a bench beneath the apple trees, but he pulled away and walked on ahead. She called to him, sat on a bench and watched his dark, retreating form against the humorous bric-a-brac of the walkway. Let him go, she said to herself. She studied the theatre. Only its gay facade remained after

78

a fire had gutted it a few years earlier, and it seemed a perfect image to her desolate thoughts. Should she go talk to Xiao Li's parents in her rudimentary Chinese? It would be like describing a computer with wooden blocks. And what about Xiao Ruyu? He loved Xiao Ruyu, she knew that. If only she could go to Xiao Ruyu and appeal to her. If only she could line up his family and Xiao Ruyu against him, if she could persuade them that it was in their interests to let him return to Canada and *then* to work for their emigration. In time he would have the best of two worlds in Kamloops.

She sat beneath the crabapple tree and inhaled its subtle aroma. The nannies had taken all their small charges home, and the foreigners were back in their rooms taking hot showers or over in the barrooms getting slowly drunk. And being a *waiguo* ghetto meant there were no young Chinese couples seeking an unlighted corner away from the prying eyes of their neighbourhood committees. So she was alone again, which seemed her natural condition in life.

It would be so easy merely to cave in to his demands, and she was constantly surprised that she hadn't already done so. Xiao Li could go back to his parents and to Xiao Ruyu, keeping up pretenses by visiting her at the hotel, and she could go on teaching at her institute year after year, a ward of the State. She hadn't this kind of security back in Kamloops, where the government had already on several occasions tried to exorcise her programs from the college. It was only a matter of time and she would join the other teachers on unemployment and eventually welfare. The Yellow Emperor had buried the Confucius scholars up to their necks in sand and lopped their heads off, but in Canada they stuck you in sand and left you there to die a natural death.

Even if she succeeded in getting Xiao Li back to Kamloops, he'd fall down in front of the television set and never get up again. Why had she insisted? She stared at the moon, which had just slipped above the flared eyes of the hotel buildings, large and orange, fiercely personal. It gave her back her thoughts, and she felt mesmerized until at last the moon was high enough to turn pale. Yes, he would go bad, and it would be her own fault.

Why not go home and leave him here? The worst that could happen to him would be political rehabilitation; he'd have to write a few self-criticisms and go to a few lectures, but in time he'd find a friend who'd show him the *houmen*, the backdoors, which would take him back to his starting point. Anyway, why had she insisted? She had asked herself that and never received a satisfactory answer. It was true that she loved him. Why did she love him? He was cold, really. He was lousy in bed, he was an alien, a recluse, he hated her country. Maybe she needed him because without him she had nobody. But with him also she had nobody. Did she feel sorry for him? Was he her charge? Did she feel responsible for him? This would make her a colonist, the very idea of which was repugnant to her. No, she would leave him to fend for himself, and she would go back and resign from the college and go out to Toronto and find a new job working for an import-export company specializing in the Far East. She would get rich and perhaps someday visit Xiao Li, just to see how he was getting on at home.

Suddenly, she felt cold.

She rose from her bench only to discover how dark it had become. She strolled slowly along the walkway and in through the orchard and across the lot to her apartment block. She would talk to Xiao Li, she would tell him to stay in China. The *fuwuyuan* sat in their little watch-room watching her as she climbed the dark stairs. She turned on the hall-lights as she went. Why did the Chinese love dark houses so much? She reached her landing and checked her mail pouch since she hadn't got a letter from anyone for two weeks.

The door was locked.

She knocked softly. It was always so embarrassing to stand outside your own room knocking at your own door. She knocked again and then took a key from her purse and opened the door. It was dark. She turned on the light. The lid to Xiao Li's chest was thrown open. She dropped her purse and walked to the sitting room, which was also dark. At the doorframe, she paused when she saw, against the light of the window, Xiao Li sitting in a chair as if deep in contemplation.

She waited for a moment as if afraid to step into his thoughts.

"Xiao Li?" she said, "I've been thinking . . ."

Silence.

"Xiao Li?"

She switched on the ceiling light.

Sprawled across the wicker chair. A large Qing dagger standing tall in the centre of his chest. A lake of blood at his feet. It was Xiao Li, and he was dead. There was no question about it. He was dead. Xiao Li was dead.

6

The eyes of the man from the Foreign Affairs Office looked out upon her. They regarded her as an example of what had already been said many times about such women. She was not so much an object of speculation as of confirmation, proof, that all such liaisons were unhealthy. Marriages between Chinese and foreigners are at best political in nature, contracted between partners who expected something out of the relationship, something that likely will ultimately be denied since the two systems are basically incompatible, and young people who think they can gain riches and security from foreigners have allowed themselves to be duped. It might well be that foreigners have money and power, but they are also deeply flawed, even ill, and anyone who touches them is likely to be badly burnt.

Xiao Li had been burnt.

Only he said, instead, "The Embassy of Canada has been informed of my government's sorrow for what has happened, Mrs. Elizabeth." The words leaked from his lips. "We accept the facts of this . . . unfortunate happening. We will not ask . . . embarrassing questions, I assure you."

"Thank you," she said. The wind had been high in the night, and all morning she had stood at the window watching the snowfall of blossoms from the trees in the courtyard. She had been surprised to discover how resigned she had become, how strong. "I have already had a visitor from the embassy."

He smiled sadly. "Well, then," he said, looking at the hardwood floor as if to find the appropriate words for the occasion, "all that is left for me to do is to discuss the matter of the . . ." He flashed his eyes at her to avoid saying the word.

"Yes," she said, "the body."

"So."

She searched for words, too. "He should be cremated, of course," she said, the words hurting her mouth as she spoke. "But . . . I don't want the ashes." The eyes of the man narrowed. "Yes, you see, I can explain." She looked across at him and realized he didn't want or need her explanation; he already knew what she was going to say, had had it explained a dozen times. "He never left China," she said, anyway. "He took his body to Canada but he left his spirit here . . . so leave his ashes with his . . . " She felt the tears begin and sought to regain control. "I mean," she said, "please arrange to have his ashes delivered to his parents."

"I'm terribly sorry," he said, and she heard a genuine note in them. "Please accept my— "

"No!" she said. "Just go."

And he went. The door closed softly, and she rose and walked to the hallway. She looked down at the chest. She would give the body back to the parents, the knives to Xiao Ruyu, and that would leave her with nothing. Perhaps it was better that way.

THE FLYING TIGER

The Ascent

With binoculars Francis Arkin studied the mountain peak and the crimson arch crowning the stone stairs that led to it. Nan Tian Men. The South Gate of Heaven. The others were already there. They had gone to Heaven in an automobile. Afterward they would go back to Beijing and tell everyone they had *climbed* the holy mountain of Taishan.

Last night he informed Xiao Liu he was going to climb it all by himself.

"Do you know how high is mountain?" Xiao Liu had said. "Five thousand step. No, Professor Arkin, you must take *mianbao* with us. I have already say to leaders at Azure Cloud Temple at top of mountain there will be eight people for lunch."

Xiao Liu was a small, delicate man, likely from the South, who, by talking loud and keeping absolute order, tried to make up for his lack of upright Han backbone. "So you see we must travel together. The hotel already pay for *mianbao*." Xiao Liu was always talking *mianbao*. *Mianbao* this and *mianbao* that. Small passenger vans which by some inscrutable twist of the imagination the Chinese thought of as resembling a loaf of bread. "I personally responsible for you, Professor. I cannot allow you climb all the way to top by yourself. This is impossible."

"Well, I am going to climb it all the way to the top by myself and that is all there is to it."

"It take you all day, Professor."

"Good."

Xiao Liu smiled shyly. He was attached to Arkins' hotel and worked for the *waiban*, an office looking after foreign experts. "You must be careful with your heart. The Heavenly Step very steep, Professor Larkin. Now is June. The sun is very hot. No hospital on Taishan."

"I'll worry about my heart and you worry about your leaders."

The other *zhuanjia* sat around a table in the hotel restaurant humoring a giggling waitress who stood tall green quart bottles of Qingdao beer in front of them. Foreign experts. It was strange to think that you could call these silly men "experts" just because they spoke their own language.

"Haven't you heard, Arkin?" said Hagstrom, the fat one who played a tuba in his toilet every night. "Sun Wukong The Monkey King returns to Taishan every Spring to look for the White Bone Ghost who is said to live under one of the bridges along the Heavenly Stairs waiting for juicy *waiguoren* like you."

"Ritter," said Arkin, ignoring Hagstrom, "you can speak monkey talk. You go tell them at the desk that I want to be awakened at five o'clock."

Ritter was a Dane. Or was he a Nordski? The Viking looked at him and said, "Personally, I think you're making a big mistake. We're supposed to do what they tell us to."

Newman said, "Oh, let him go. Arkin's old enough to be able to know what he wants to do." Newman was a hermit, coming out of his room only for meals and then taking a table all by himself. "Why does everyone have to do what everyone else does?"

"Thank you, Newman," said Arkin. Xiao Liu had settled in between Ritter and Hagstrom. "I work for your side, Mr. Liu. I have a worker's card. I'm not just a tourist. This is not a tour. I support the Revolution. I support the Leadership. It is not against the law for a *waiguoren* to climb Taishan all by himself. In fact, it is a duty." The word *waiguoren* always made Xiao Liu's flesh crawl, and so Arkin used it whenever he wanted to win an argument. Liu had been to

Toronto and New York and understood fully how *waiguoren* never wanted to be called *waiguoren* because it somehow meant alien, with all the bad connotations. "Anyway," he said, "I didn't come to China to be a tourist. If I wanted to be herded around and shown the things the government wants me to see, not what I want to see, then I would've paid my crummy $4000 to do it. I've worked for you for almost a year now. The least you can do is let me climb the mountain all by myself."

"Don't get lost," said Newman.

"That's just what I aim to do."

Xiao Liu stared at him. He knew English; he just didn't know what Arkin meant. It was a warm June morning on the western slope of Taishan, the Holy Mountain of Shandong. The poetry of the mountain range reminded Arkin of a Ming painting: one lavender mystic mountain rising pale behind the next purplish mountain, antique verdure and thin washes, prismatic, verdant, amethyst, ghostly, jagged heights where myth and reality were lost in fog. The rugged canyons were forested by pine and juniper and pear and fir, pinnacles in the shape of messages from prehistory, and crests, ridges, waterfalls. Visible, like a silver thread, the winding stone Heavenly Stairs led to the magnificent South Gate of Heaven. Pilgrims came from all over China to be the first in the country to see the sunrise and perhaps find the magic pools in which, it was said, swam codfish over 10,000 years old, and which, if eaten, would confer immortality, or stroll about the magic orchard where, it was alleged, flowered a pear tree that bore fruit containing the elixir of everlasting life.

Yet this morning only a few pilgrims struggled along the path. Most of them were old and seemed more interested in staring at him than fishing for magic codfish. Some of the old folk sat fanning themselves on benches beneath cinnamon trees and watching him pole his way upward past the Heavenly Queen's Pool and through the First Celestial Gate and the Gate of the Heavenly Stair. They talked about him after he left. They said he was very tall. Like a god. They said in his pouch he carried magical instruments that would direct him to the ancient pools and the sacred orchards. He did, in fact, carry some fairly sophisticated hardware: ship binoculars, a map of Tai'an, a phrase book, aspirin, heart pills, a couple of ham sandwiches and three candy bars, a Swiss Army Knife and a rechargeable flashlight. The old people studied him when he stopped to buy a bottle of yellow, warm, tasteless *qishui* and gathered at his feet when he sat to drink it beneath the dry pine trees. The eyes were fixed upon him. He had read where they were not being rude, only curious. They hadn't seen too many foreigners because it had been only six years since the Downfall of The Gang of Four. The book said all you had to do was smile at them and say something in their own tongue and they'd go away out of a sense of embarrassment at hearing a *waiguoren* murdering the language.

"*Ni hao!*" he barked, smiling. "*Zenmeyang?*"

It didn't work.

"*Nimen chi le ma?*"

They kept right on staring at him as if he had two heads or had grown an extra ear in the middle of his nose.

He should have gotten used to it by now. He'd been in China for seven months. Seven months! He should have gotten used to a lot of things. But nothing had changed. He was still the same old fart who grasped at any chance to get out of town. Straws, he was used to grasping at straws. He was 55 years old. Nobody had wanted him around. His wife was dead, his children driven into divorce and unemployment compensation. He had been told he was redundant in the only work he knew how to do and they had given him early retirement to get him out of the way. But he had nothing to retire to. It was that simple. Someone told him about teaching in China, and Arkin jumped at the chance because he had been to China during the War and remembered it as a time when he believed in everything. Now he believed in nothing. Since the war he'd had the feeling his leaky lifeboat was becalmed in a bay of sharks.

Small kids living in the brick yards along Taishan's holy path came out to watch him. Unbelievably beautiful children, delicate, like carved ivory offerings to the gods. And an old woman with bound feet— they called the packaged feet 'golden lilies', can you imagine?— came out and teetered before him, holding a golden child on her hip and pointing a long, bony finger and saying, "*Waiguoren! Waiguoren!*"

At Hong Men Gong, Palace of the Red Gate, Francis Arkin took out his binoculars again and looked up at Heaven's gate. It seemed now farther off. Even inaccessible. Arkin took out his handkerchief, wiped his face and sat on a low stone wall well worn. Likely they had all sat here before setting off on the long upward scale of philosophic heights: Qing Shi Huang di, Confucius, Kubla Khan, Qianlong, Chiang Kai-shek, Chairman Mao, Zhou Enlai, Deng Xiaoping . . . likely they felt the soreness at having climbed to this point and looked up at Heaven's gate. Did it seem farther off to them? Were they, like him, clutching at straws?

What he worried about was coming back down. He knew he could climb the mountain, but what would it be like, coming down not having found the eternal codfish?

He set off again. Path led on to path, which, in turn led on to still other paths, and it was nearly noon before he realized that he was no longer climbing, that, in fact, if anything, he was descending again to the common plain. It was the story of his life. Another disappointment. Another failure. He took out his binoculars and focussed them on the mountain.

The South Gate of Heaven had utterly vanished.

The Descent

The children saw it first.

They came to the edge of the village to watch. Yes, it came straight out of the mountain just as the old people said it would and it walked in a strange way, and when it stumbled and fell, it uttered words they had never heard before. The old folks, having missed the children, came to look for them and found them standing together at the edge of the fields watching something come straight out of the mountain and across the fields. The road from Tai'an, the old ones knew, came from the opposite direction, and if anyone ever came to visit, they came along that road. This one came from the road down the mountain. But they worried less about the direction than about the way it stumbled across the fields, as if it had never before walked on level ground. The children and the old folk shared the same spectrum of the imagination, and they also knew that they lived in a village nobody ever visited. It was a village without strangers. Puzhao was famous in history, but history had gone away. That was what Lao Jiang had said. Lao Jiang had been in the town since the Northern Expeditionary Army came through fighting the Japanese invaders. And so Lao Jiang had to be the first to say it. "*Waiguoren,*" she said, and they all nodded in silent assent. They stood together watching, and Lao Wang, considered the second wisest person in the village, said, "*Dui. Waiguoren.*" And then they all said it, "*Waiguoren.*"

In time the foreigner climbed the last irrigation ditch like, they thought, a spider and came to the rutted road that ringed the old village. The birds along the roadway set up a horrid chatter and flew off. The Children pressed back until they found the hard knees of the elders, and together the old and the young watched the foreigner come.

He stopped when he reached them and took off his floppy grey hat and, with his long nose and skyblue eyes, leaned down to Ni Baolong's Xiao Ni. He had, of course, that soft flowing white hair that looked like clouds and that forehead as large as an ocean and that long white beard that pointed straight into your eyes. They saw the backpack and thought they would now see the fuzzy epidermis of the immortal peach or the flashing silver scales of the immortal fish which, it is said, wise men bore from the mountain top.

"Do you speak English, my man?" he said.

At which the boy fled, flashing feet along the road into the village and without looking back.

Arkin stepped forward, took off his hat and said, "I am Francis Arkin. I am a teacher at one of your noble universities, the Institute of Mechanical Engineering." He fixed his eyes upon an old man naked to the waist, skin the shimmer of polished brass, bearing a small bronze baby with porcelain

eyes, round pools of wonder, enchanted, and then he turned
to smile at an old woman too old for her age, with sunstruck
and suspicious eyes, face the color of a saddle, but with feet
carbuncular and legs worn and sanded.

"I am lost," he said. "I set out to climb Taishan, but I
seem to have come to your village instead." They simply
stared at him. "Don't worry, I've been to your country before.
I was in the war against the Japanese. I was an aeronautical
mechanic. I came over here with General Claire Chennault.
Remember Claire Chennault? The Flying Tigers? The funny
airplanes with the dragon's jaw painted over the cowling?"
They weren't much for talking. "I used to work on them.
Sometimes I flew in them, too. Now, look, I can't stay long. I'm
not even supposed to be here. They don't want me here. Is
there anybody in your town who speaks English?" He tried
his few ragged phrases. *"Hui bu hui yingyu?"* Still no response. Maybe they didn't speak Mandarin either. "Okay,
then what I want is for you to go inside the village and fetch
out your oldest and wisest man, someone my age, and we can
have a talk without having my bosses or yours hanging over
us listening to what we say." They looked hypnotized. "Look,
I'm real tired. I got to go find some place to sit down and get
out of this heat."

But they only stared at him.

So he walked toward the village, and the kids and the
old ones followed at his heels like an obedient dust cloud. The
village was mean. Reality was never what it was cracked up
to be. He walked down what was a mere open sewer between
two brick walls. There was no In and no Out, no main street,
no town center, nothing much more than a collection of walls
and brickmud houses and piles of horseshit and narrow
lanes, rutted and muddy, and a strange commingling of
unfortunate odors.

He walked until he found a bench tilting up against
one of the brick walls and out of the sun. He fell onto it and
dropped his knapsack in front of his feet. He was tired. The
old and the young he had been towing in from the edge of the
village now stood gathered around him without saying a
word, and they would have remained in that position until

89

nightfall, had not, suddenly, the middle-aged ones, the mothers and fathers, the storekeepers, the bookkeepers, the shitscrapers, come out of their workshops and houseyards to see the old folk and the children staring at a *waiguoren* sitting on a bench. Being responsible persons, of course, they refused to panic. Something had to be done. They sent someone to find Lao Xu, who was chairman of the production team. He would know what to do.

Francis Arkin held the tired globe of head in his hands and tried to regain his composure.

"I apologize," he said to them. "I should have told you I was coming. But even if I had been able to write, they wouldn't have let me mail it." More and more people came running into the road. "You and I live in two different worlds. First and Third. There just isn't any way we can ever meet unless we escape our keepers. Okay, I know I'm not supposed to be here. And I know you're worried and embarrassed about your ugly little town, but it doesn't really matter, see? *Nimen bu hui, wo bu hui.* You live only once, don't you? Whatever happened? Once upon a time we got along. I used to fly out of Kunming and up to Chongqing regular. I was a mechanic. There were lots of us. Hell, I knew most of the pilots in the sky over China. And you know what? I loved every one of them. They were real heroes in my book."

He wanted to go lie down somewhere. He took one of his heart pills and swallowed it dry. He needed to take a short nap to collect his wits and convert a genuine mistake into something he could talk about when he went home. It was a chance to meet some real Chinese people, not the stooges they designed for him, not the puppets, the clones, the spokesmen. This was a real village, not one of the model villages out behind the model production units behind model communities.

God, he was tired! He had to lie down. "Now, look," he said, "I'm just going to take myself a little *xiuxi,* if you don't mind." He smiled and stretched out across the bare wooden bench and pulled his hat over his eyes.

Something sailed through the air and fell close to the bench. He sat up and lifted his hat. A brick lay at his feet.

Along the road he heard the pitchpuzzle voices, the anger and the yammer. He struggled to his feet and punched a hole through the crowd and came to the open gate where he saw them beating the boy. He jumped among them and snatched the victim from their hands, thrusting himself in front like a shield. "No!" he screamed. "Leave him! He didn't mean to hurt me!" The people in the courtyard seemed hurt by his voice. "People from my part of the world have been throwing stones at him for a couple centuries and now it's his turn!"

But the boy struggled free and turned and buried a fist into Arkin's stomach and then ran out past the amazed onlookers and down the street. Arkin fell to his knees and his stomach broke like a glass bottle. A man came, younger and stronger than the others. He talked loudly and made some youths pick the foreigner up and support him and they walked him into the house, and then they placed him onto a bed. All Arkin wanted to do was sleep for a while and think about things.

The Crash

When he awoke, he found himself lying in a cool white-washed bed chamber. A young girl was perched on a high stool staring at him from the middle of the room, her hands folded like flowers in her lap. She wore a neat light-blue dress. A red bandanna was tied about her long, thin neck. She had the bright searching eyes of a scholar and possessed the backbone of a soldier. When he spoke, she refused to flinch.

He said: "Hello, young lady. Who are you?"

"My name is Sun Lili," she pronounced her words with schoolroom precision. " But my English is very bad."

"Your English is excellent."

She shook her head and her pig-tails uncoiled and flew about her head like small black snakes. "No, my English is v-e-r-y bad!"

"I'm going to call you 'Lily' because it's close to your name. How old are you, Lily?"

"I am twelve years old."

"My name is Francis and I am 55 years old." She seemed to understand. "How is it you speak English?"

"I visit my . . . grandmother. He live here."

"Your grandmother is a woman. A woman is 'she'. Where do you live?"

"Tianjin."

She smiled awkwardly and, as she spoke, she swung her body about in a nervous circle. Francis Arkin tried to sit up on the bed, but his head ached and he felt dizzy.

"Now, Lily, I want you to go out and find someone my age. Tell him I was in the war. Tell him we were comrades together. Tell him I want to talk with him. Tell him I have a lot to say." The girl stared at him, her eyes growing wider the longer he spoke. "Aren't you following me?"

"Yes," she said, weakly. "You are sick. You want go home."

"No. I want to meet a man."

"A man?"

"Someone like me. An old man! Someone in the war."

"War!"

He went through the motions of shooting guns and dropping bombs and dying. He felt especially gifted at the moment with the dying part. "War, you see?"

"Yes, I see. War."

"Bring him here. I want to talk to him."

But she only stared at him.

"Go!" he said and the girl fled, slamming the door behind her. Francis Arkin climbed across a straw tick and looked out the window. The entire village stood massed in the road watching the building in which the stranger had been placed. Was it this way when Marco Polo came to the *hutongs* of Dadu? Had the Han stood about like this, studying the tall, white, hairy body and the long nose and round eyes of the *waiguoren* as he moved toward the high golden throne of Kubla Khan? Four hundred years had come and gone and still the occidental race remains an object of wonder and delight to the Chinese people, who by now like the rest of the world should have discovered its abject mediocrity.

He went back to his pillow and buried his frail

remains beneath the comforter. It was a narrow room with a *k'ang*, a high brick bed, on one side and a file of shiny drawers and chairs and small tables on the other. Doilies over everything. And on top of the dresser were two hideous red vases and two bouquets of hideous shiny flowers, and on the walls a portrait of The Smiling Chairman and three framed certificates for some kind of heroics covered with red stars and ribbons and scrawled signatures. The floor was grey painted concrete, the walls and ceiling white-washed plaster, and the green curtains had a print of bamboo and panda bears. Why was it they always locked you away behind walls? The Chinese always found you a room somewhere, a good room, and considered it polite to lock you away from the rest of the people.

The door to the bedroom opened and in walked Lily, drawing behind her a small old bald man with a frizzled white beard. He wore a long bleach-blue peasant's coat, patched and repatched in various hues of blue, and he dragged himself across the floor in a pair of worn black cotton shoes. His eyes were hidden deep in fleshy sockets and appeared not to be able to see anything. His wrinkled old face looked like a map of the universe as he walked toward Arkin carrying a steaming bowl of rice with something green and slimy dumped over the top of it. Chopsticks had been driven into the skull of the rice.

He spoke in Chinese and handed it to Arkin.

"Thank you," said Arkin. "*Xie Xie!*"

"This man name Lao Dong," said Lily.

"*Ni hao*, Lao Dong."

"*Ni hao.*" The old man smiled, and there was in that smile something authentic, a form of communication. But what was it saying? Most Chinese people smiled graciously when you met them, but in this old man's kind face was something more. Something of recognition, perhaps. He had a strong suspicion that he was not the first American Lao Dong had ever met.

"Lao Dong, war. He soldier."

"Tell him I was a soldier, too."

She told him, and he laughed out loud.

"Tell him I was in the Flying Tigers."

The girl only stared at him. "Frying tigers?" she said, amused. "Tigers not fry."

"During the war I was in an airplane . . ." Arkin made wings with his hands and sketched the essence of airplane, droning and making sibilance with his breath. They both laughed at him. "Lily, get me paper and pencil." She knew more English than she let on: she went to the dresser and returned with precisely what he wanted. "Thank you, Lily. You are indeed a scholar." He drew a picture of a P-40, and when he added the gaping dragon's jaw, Lao Dong laughed even harder.

"Yes, yes!" Lily said, squirming on her seat. "Lao Dong know Frying Tiger."

"What army was he in?" But Lily only stared. "What army? Army?" He made as if shooting a rifle. "What army?"

They talked for a while, and then the girl said, "Red Army."

He talked about himself. It seemed necessary. And it all came naturally, with complication, rising action, crisis and denouement. He had never before considered his life as something that had form, plot, action in which he was a principal player, as something accomplished. Things had happened. He had been an object shoved about by forces. The dates and events of his life but hasty entries in a black-and-white curriculum vitae.

She sat now on the edge of the bed, closer, more relaxed, and as he spoke, she spun the words out before her to Lao Dong as if writing on a slate in her schoolroom. He had to repeat himself many times, but the main plot was there, the characters, the theme. And all the while he talked, he watched Lao Dong's face. This had been an intelligent soldier, a man who knew things, remembered names, battles, and often seemed even a little bored with the memory of it. Arkin told Lily to tell Lao Dong that he was sorry about what happened after the war and that, if it had been up to him, he would have made sure that his country had backed the winners.

"I have told him my story, Lily," he said. "Now ask him

to tell me his."

The two of them talked for a while; Lao Dong shook his head many times, but then held up his hand and gazed for some time at the floor. After a long silence, he began to talk and the girl spoke slowly and often interrupted the old man when she could not understand him.

"The Japan soldier come and shoot guns to grandmother and grandfather," she said. "They put a gun knife into top of head of he brother and sister. Two sister. Sister have baby in stomach. They kill baby too. Kill all baby. All old people. Then they put baby and old people into ground. Lao Dong run away. Hide long time. No eat. He come to Hebei. He join army and fight Japan soldier. Japan soldier burn down fields. Burn houses and trees. Lao Dong shoot in night only. No bullets. He make bullets. Chinese soldier make bullets. Some not good. Soldier shoot self. Japanese hide bomb in rice field. After war baby step on bomb. Baby die."

Words out of the mouth of a child. They stung him in their uncanny accuracy. She was a poet with *his* language.

"Lao Dong say he see many airplanes. America airplanes. They friend to China. Sometime they shoot gun. Sometime they fall to earth."

The story wound about him like a deadly serpent, and he felt himself squeezed into mourning for burning children and starving soldiers, and when the old man went silent, Arkin threw the covers back and sat on the edge of the bed; Lao Dong got up from his chair and laughed.

He wanted to ask Lao Dong more questions, but shouting broke out in the road. The crowd had broken up. It was drifting down the road. Something coming toward them. A car. A long black car with red flags flying from its glossy front fenders. The car slowed as it approached the village. The people gathered around it. The girl saw the car too. She said something to Lao Dong and pointed toward the car and Lao Dong jumped off the stool and began to chatter anxiously as he squared his little blue cap to his bald head, and then he turned and walked quickly toward the back door of the room.

"Lao Dong say you come," she said, putting her body up against his to help him to his feet. There was an animal strength inside those narrow, bronze joints. "He show you. He want you see."

The three of them walked out into a garden and left by a back gate. The lane was empty. They hurried as fast as two old men could go, one of whom was driven along by a young girl who came barely to his armpit. At last they reached a narrower lane that shot off at an angle toward the distant hills. An old woman stood in one of the gates watching them. Lao Dong stopped and spoke wildly to her, and she ran back into the yard. Arkin was already tired. He had forgotten his camera. He had forgotten his knapsack. His pills. He felt nauseous, confused, lost.

"Where are we going?"

Behind them Arkin heard loud voices, doors being slammed, people running through the streets. The old rutted road curved beneath the bony trees and into hot, dusty bush land until it came to an old wooden wall, once painted and decorated with posts and statues, but now all in a heap but for the tall high, red, sagging gateway that leaned in against itself, barely visible among the thick cedar trees. The cicadas split Arkin's ears, and so the commotion back in the village was lost. Arkin felt he was on an expedition, and he was certain of one thing— not too many *waiguoren* had ever been in these backwoods.

But he was wrong. Lao Dong waited for them at the gateway, and together, the girl on one side, the old man on the other, they steered Arkin across what appeared once to have been a garden. The pools were dry now and the trees withered and fruitless. High weeds obscured the distances, and tilting and weathered sandstone statues of warriors and priests and mythological beasts peered at them from the darkness, and when the three of them reached the far end of the graveyard, Lao Dong dropped to his knees and with his old hands began to brush the debris from the ground. Dead grass, boards and bottles seemed to have purposefully been piled there. Gradually, what emerged was a piece of granite laid flat across the earth.

Something was written on it. Something in English. "See!" said Lily.

He fell to his knees beside Lao Dong and stared at it. Lao Dong looked at him and began to speak in a peculiar way, his eyes flung open, the nostrils flared, the teeth flashing in the light. Lily merely stood back staring at Lao Dong. Her eyes were filled with terror as she whispered something to herself.

Arkin brushed the sand from the letters on the stone. A man's name.

ANDREW MILLR.
U.S. ARMY AIR CORS.
YEAR 1943.

Words written by a hand that did not write English words. Words read by tired old eyes, letters left out in the writing because of old bony hands and poor light. Time had worn the words but not erased them, and wars and civil commotions and cultural revolutions and rainstorms and winds had not moved the stone.

"Lao Dong say nobody know he . . . this stone here," said Lily. She smiled at the old man. "I know not, too."

"Miller . . . Miller," said Arkin, throwing his head back and staring up through the trees at the everblue Shandong sky. "Oh my God! Miller!"

Someone was coming up the road.

Lao Dong grunted and struggled to his feet and stared at Arkin, and he and Lily tried to lift him to his feet.

"We go now!" said Lily. "We go now!"

But the *waiguoren* was as heavy as the tombstone he stared at.

Lao Dong scuffed the sand and grass back over the stone and walked back toward the gate. Lily tried once more to lift Arkin by the arm, but he pushed her gently away. She went and stood beside Lao Dong at the gate. The car came up the road toward the graveyard, rolling slowly, towing a cloud of townspeople with it, but Arkin, bent over the grave, heard or saw nothing. He was remembering how Miller used to eat his peas with chopsticks: there was a jeweller's fastidiousness about it, a theatrical precision as he plucked the little round green pearl out of the rice and twirled it in the air and cradled it on his tongue while he made clucking noises with his throat and crossed his eyes and stared at you like Ben Blue.

SUMMIT

The day began. Much like all the others.

The *fuwuyuan* were up early because really there wasn't a lot to do and they wanted to get it done so they could get down to the business of drinking tea and reading old newspapers. Loudspeakers at a school bordering the hotel yarred and yapped and then came the small snarling garden tractors manned by panda-fat workmen wearing blue horse-blankets and rolling through the hotel roads hauling sour vegetables and broken brick into the countryside.

Newman donned his yellow house-gown and went for a walk along the dark corridors. He was escaping from a stack of papers written by students who handled ideas as if they were large, bulky objects that had to be set down somewhere, and fast.

His rooms were at the top of Building Four, a grey pile of stones far from the solemn lobbies and faded concourses made lurid by small electric light bulbs. In fact, Newman lived in the last rooms in the last hotel in a compound of dark and lifeless hotels behind walls and gates that faced a road running up from the Forbidden City to the Summer Palace, a stretch of concrete bloodied with centuries of revolution, war and traffic accidents.

On the top floor there were only the two rooms. They faced each other. Number 4616 was now empty. Its brass digits glared at him when he returned and he paused to glare back. In fact, he glared at them so long, they began moving! He hurried, then, to his own room, but before he shut the door he saw two *fuwuyuan* emerging from 4616, carrying brooms.

The rooms across the hallway had lain empty ever since Janet Sellors departed. Newman had had a brief, unproductive relationship with Janet Sellors, who had come to China to teach international economics but quickly discovered she would be treated like so many pounds of human flesh. She lasted but two months and then informed her *danwei* she wanted to go home. They told her since she had broken the contract, she'd have to pay her own way back, and Janet told them an airline ticket was likely the best investment she had ever made. "My mother used to warn me when I was a little girl not to dig too deeply in my sandbox because I might just fall out into China," she cried to Newman. "I wish it had been that easy. I spent my whole life trying to get here and now I find it's just like Akron." Janet had tried to lift the Dostoevskian veils of her rooms with bright prints and scrolls of calligraphy, but when she returned to Ohio, she left them all behind. The *fuwuyuan* came and removed them, of course, and restored the rooms to their former crespuscular solemnities.

Ah, well! Now at least he would not be all alone.

The new neighbour was a tall, grey man in a tall, grey hat of fur, and Newman knew at once he was a Russian. He nodded briefly to the man as he entered Janet's rooms, but there was little to recommend itself as acknowledgement other than perhaps a slight stiffening of lips, as if the teeth held back words that might have been uttered but for the even greyer man behind him. Newman nodded to him as well, but the second man— short, balding, with thick spectacles— regarded Newman as a form of threat to human life itself.

Newman closed the door and went to a window. He looked out across the roofs of the dusty sheds that stretched out in a haze toward the mountains that stood in the middle of a long, dry land stretching north by northwest into the forbidden distances that came out at the Siberian extremities. It was a view which often confirmed to Newman that he lived in the oldest and dustiest cities in a world of such distances and dimensions that it had posed the ultimate questions about human existence and had never received sufficient answers to them. Newman took out his violin and worked on it for an hour or so in order to forget the pile of student essays and the hotel and the new neighbor and, of course, his lost life, his vanished wife and his faded career. The violin had saved him in the past, and it would save him in the future. He was not a good violinist, but he was a competent one. He had studied the violin all his life and had, from time to time, achieved a modicum of success with it, but it had never become an occupation with him. He was an English professor even if, for the present, he didn't have a post and hadn't, indeed, had one since 1975. He stood in the center of one of his two rooms and stared at himself in the long mirror on the door of the commode. He liked to watch himself as he played because he wanted to maintain a look of composure and good posture even as he executed the more difficult passages of the Mozart he was working on. What he saw there in the mirror was one George Newman, Ph.D., University of Oregon, 1967, a tall, grey eminence with a short, chiselled chin and gremlin eyes, a nose a trifle too large for the face. He had a little difficulty with one of the passages but maintained his composure even as he marvelled at his inability to master the work of a man who lived two hundred fifty years earlier and who by the time he reached George Newman's age had already been dead for twenty years. Mozart was of course a god, but Newman had been forced to accept the fact that he himself was every inch an ordinary man.

At noon he had read through only half of the papers and came down with a headache. He took two aspirin and went to lunch.

Locking his door, he turned to observe the darkness of the door across the way. They had taken off the cheery ornaments that had been pinned to it to dispell the gloom. He laughed at his own joke. It was, after all, only poetic justice. The Russians had built the hotel back in the 1950s when they believed they were achieving the Millenium in Asia, but only a decade went by and the Chinese told them to go home again.

The darknesses of the hotel remained, and now that the Russians were coming back, it was only fitting that they reinherited their own gloom.

Newman walked down the steps and through the lobby, and the *fuwuyuan* stood about logging his passage. Meiguoren. Room 4616. 12:05. To Number Eight dining room. Expected return, one o'clock. Were they watching the Russian so carefully?

It was a week before Newman saw him again.

This time there were two fat and ugly, two gold-toothed and near-sighted women who waddled along behind him as if they owned the goddamn hotel. Newman heard them talking behind the door. One had a flat voice in which her words exploded like land mines, and she ended her sentences with a low growl. The other hung out words as if they were flags flapping in a bright spring wind. The two of them seemed to speak to each other, though there were long silences which, presumably, were the man's contribution. The women left and Newman went to the door, leaning close. It was silent in the room for a long time, and eventually Newman went to bed. He left the door ajar all the following days, but there seemed to be no comings and goings, other than the occasional visit of the two women, gold teeth flashing, who filled the room with cackle and clatter.

Newman never heard his neighbor laugh, he never heard him cry. He heard nothing at all from him for about a month and then, suddenly one night, he heard the cello.

The Russian played a magnificent cello. The notes were secure, absolute, the tone mature, rich, the expression rounded with the ardor of conviction and experience. At first Newman speculated that the man was a professional musician who had come to teach the Chinese how to play the cello. Everyone was talking about rapprochement, now they were doing something about it. Yet, curiously, the man never took the cello from his room. Newman watched him leave the building, saw him climb into taxis, but the Russian never took the cello with him. Perhaps he had another one somewhere. That seemed unlikely. Maybe he was a spy. The Russians were coming back, they'd have to bring the KGB with them, wouldn't they? So that was it: this guy was a KGB agent who kept his eyes on the old birds who, presumably, taught Russian at one of the institutes. There were always three. One to watch the other and the third to watch the other two. So this was The Third Man.

Knowing this, Newman avoided the man in the hallways, passing him without acknowledgement, watching him from the cave of his doorway— always there was the slight, sideways flick of the eyes, the escape.

Well, Newman would practice the Cold War on him. Not because he was a believer, but because it seemed most natural. After all, they had been bitter enemies now for forty years. It was something understood, a studied and brutal, sullen dehumanization. Once as a student at Oberlin, he had met a Russian exchange student who was a carbon copy of himself. They sat together in a large lecture room outfitted like the United Nations General Assembly, and the Russian got up to speak about the American intervention in Lebanon. When he sat down again, he looked at Newman and smiled savagely, but his eyes said, Why are we terrorizing each other like this? Newman thought to indicate he understood but was amazed to discover he was quite capable of holding his face in a mask of supreme indifference.

The cello was, however, something else.

It struck without warning. It eluded all his defenses and swept down upon him, leaving him helpless.

Newman met the Russian at the entrance to Building Four in the revolving door.

Their eyes met and for a moment the two of them were locked together in the rotating glass wheel. They were, however, forced to cooperate by pushing in opposite directions in order to gain their freedom from each other.

November blew out of Siberia and became December.

"I play Voice of America at him," he told Sid Weeks and his wife, "and he plays Radio Moscow at me." He had only a few friends in spite of the neighborhood, for the hotel was like a ghetto, admittedly fur-lined. They drank cheap Chinese brandy and whispered as if someone had them surrounded. "Only thing is he's got a regular loudspeaker for a radio and he always plays it LOUD."

"Does the guy speak English?" asked Sid.

"How should I know?"

"Well," said Nan Weeks, "do you speak Russian?"

"Absolutely not."

"Luck of the draw," said Sid. "The lady in the apartment above us is from somewhere in the Middle East and prefers to grind out her early morning breakfasts in mortar and pestle right above our head."

"Anyway," said his wife, "now you've got a perfect excuse to go on ignoring one another."

"I can't ignore him! I mean, well . . . here I am stuck with this guy miles from anybody else and all alone in the dark."

"He plays the cello."

"Unfortunately."

"Mmmm!" said Sid, puffing contentedly upon an old knobby pipe that always stank up Newman's room so badly that it took a week afterwards to fully air it out. "Why don't the two of you get together?" Sid Weeks was a Canadian and of course couldn't fully appreciate the intricacies of American-Russian relationships. "I mean, didn't Mozart write anything for violin and cello?"

"Seems such a reasonable combination," said his wife.

"Composers always put a whole lot of instruments in between the two."

"Well, get up a quartet and ask him to play cello."

They left, but the thought hung about in the stale smoke. Newman opened the window, but the smoke and the thought clung. A closet violinist, he preferred to play to his own reflection in the mirror, and, indeed, about a week later, observing his posture carefully, he was once again shocked and discomforted. It was the cello alright, but there was something more . . . it was a whole damn quartet coming out of the Russian's rooms. The two violins were slavish and weak and the violist was *mamahuhu*. The Cellist was, however, divine. The Russian carried the quartet on his back. Shostakovitch, maybe. Something gloomy, awesome, something breathless and frightening, dark.

The quartet met Wednesdays.

The rest of the week the Russian sat silent in his rooms. Never practiced once, never ran the scales. Newman, on the other hand, played every night, played up a storm. The Russian would have to understand that Newman was an articulate musician, well-read and versatile. In the middle of his recital, however, often his neighbor's radio would suddenly erupt and drown him out. He played Mozart and Haydn, Purcell, lots and lots of Bach. It was all full of divine light, it was intellectual, free-thinking, it was a counterbalance to the heavy, plodding Russian music that Wednesdays clouded the hallways.

Confronted with Radio Moscow, Newman would drop the violin and turn on VOA as loud as it would go.

He needed his own quartet.

The hotel of course was full of people who played instruments— a noisy jazz saxophonist, a clarinetist, a pianist or two, a couple of rock guitarists. None of them would do. He needed serious musicians.

He'd have to go out to the conservatory. He knew one guy, Lu Jian. Played bassoon. He went out there one afternoon and put it to him that he needed some musicians and he needed them on Tuesdays. One day, he calculated, before the Russian. Oh, one thing more: they had to speak English. His Chinese was child's talk. Lu Jian introduced him to a violist, Li something, who smiled and said, sure, he'd bring along a violinist and a cellist and they'd make music together.

On Tuesday, they came as promised. He watched them walk into his rooms and sit in a circle and knew he had made a serious mistake. Two of them had been the very musicians whom he had seen going into the Russian's rooms.

"Do you know him?" said Newman, pointing his bow toward the Russian's room. "You play with him. I know, I saw you going over there last week."

"We know him," said Li. Newman would call him 'Xiao Li', Little Li. The others were Xiao Hu and Xiao Hui. "He good. He werry good. You play . . . at him?"

"No," said Newman. He smiled at Xiao Li's minor error. "No, I do not play with him. Perhaps . . . against him."

Li did not understand. They hacked away at the music for an hour and a half, and when at last they packed up and went down the hallway, Newman sang out the farewells much louder than he needed to. He looked across the hall at the Russian's door. It wasn't ajar. It wasn't even locked. It was bolted solid, and it was as dark as the night. There wasn't even a small light at the bottom of the door to admit of curiosity.

January, February. Newman's institute took its annual Spring Holiday, and Newman went to Guilin and down the Lijiang River. He knew he was as close to heaven as he was ever going to get; afterward, he flew to Guangzhou in an old airplane without seatbelts and prayed he would come no closer to hell. Guangzhou was dirty and everyone had his hand in one of Newman's pockets. It was a kind of caveman capitalism, and he imagined himself a wild, hunted animal. Even his Chinese money wasn't any good. "Waihui! Waihui!" they shouted at him from the rooftops, demanding foreign exchange certificates. He had, among all his other cards, a small white one which was supposed to tell everybody that he, Newman, was one of them, that he had thrown away one year of his life to lend a hand to the modernization of the country, but often the shopkeepers would only stare at the card as if it were part of a plot on the part of Beijing to stop them from making money. It seemed he always had the wrong papers on him. At the border, for instance, he was sent into a small room where a man asked him why he hadn't brought his customs declaration.

"My what?" he said.

"You are required," said the official, "to present your custom's declaration."

"I don't have one."

"When you come to China, you fill in one of this declarations."

He handed a form to Newman.

"That one? I don't remember that one."

"Please to fill it out," said the official, wisely.

Hongkong, he thought, was sprung like a delicate silver timepiece. He went everywhere by computer card, and store clerks approached him, saying, "Excuse me, sir, may I help you?" Often Newman forgot where he was and turned, thinking they were talking to someone behind him. He ate Mexican food, bought a camera, saw a movie and finished off a perfect day with a banana split.

He even watched a spaghetti western all the way to the final shoot-down.

The last day in the silver city he bought the score to the Borodin quartet he had heard coming from the Russian's apartment. He had no intention of playing it himself; he was only curious whether the Russian was actually playing the notes that the composer had placed upon the page.

Then, he went back inside.

He took a train from Guangzhou to Beijing and found himself in a soft-sleeper compartment with three heavy smokers. They were cadres from the Ministry of Trade, plain, ordinary men, basically honest and friendly, and they practiced their English upon him until he found refuge in the corridor, where he sat at a small table and read through the Borodin. How clever it all was, how light down there beneath the gloom, yes there was music inside it. The problem had been the Chinese musicians. They hadn't understood. It was all in their fingers, not in their nerves, sinew and flesh. There, he and the Russian shared something the Chinese would never be able to share, something about history, the human spirit in chains, the Indo-European bio-psychology. Newman gazed out upon the empty countryside and wondered whether the Russians, when they lived in China, had ever looked out train windows and felt, like him, a visitor from another planet.

"You like China?" asked one of his room-mates.

"I like the people," he said, evasively.

"Do you like China food?"

"Yes," he said. He tried to remember what Chinese food tasted like. "But I don't like the oil and the monosodium-glutamate."

They stared at each other. The words hadn't appeared anywhere in their readers. One of them pulled a small dictionary from his pocket and began to look up the word. "We have very good Chinese food in San Francisco."

"How old are you?" said the timid one.

"Fifty-one."

They smiled at each other. "We are surprised," said the thin man. "I say you only thirty."

"How many children?"

"None. I'm not married now."

"That too bad," said the old man, who had not yet spoken. It was time to utter truths. "A man must have children."

He made arrangements with Xiao Li. But when Tuesday rolled around, he found only two of them at his door.

"Hello," he said. "Where's Xiao Hu?"

"I am sorry," said Xiao Li, "but, you see, Xiao Hu's mother is sick. She . . . he go to countryside to visit her." Newman tried to look sympathetic but it was a real let-down. "He cannot come."

"That's too bad."

"Sorry."

"How long will he be gone?"

"I do not know," said Xiao Li. He wore western clothing and long silken hair, and he was a handsome boy. Newman stared at his friend. Xiao Hui was, on the other hand, a sad, undernourished and frightened youth, and Newman felt there was only a vague sense of himself. Xiao Hui often looked at Newman as one who had listened carefully to his elders when they talked about foreigners. They were, of course, never to be trusted because they had always ganged up on China and always would do so.

"Now we are only a trio," said Newman.

"We need cello," said Xiao Li, looking suddenly toward the Russian's room.

"No!" said Newman. Too quickly. He grabbed hold of his violin and wheeled away at it to still his pounding heart. It was too early. He wasn't ready. It was up to the Russian to invite him over. Why should he be the first to make a move? It might be dangerous. Why give him the advantage? It was far better like this, to sit near each other and to ignore, knowing all the while that should one or the other of them move, there might be repercussions. "No," he said again, "I will not go and ask him."

"I will go," said Xiao Li.

"You?"

"Yes, I will go. I will try my best."

Xiao Li straightened himself and marched across the hallway and up to the Russian's door and tapped upon it. The great door spun slowly inward upon its iron wrists and out of the blank white light emerged the shadow of a tall man with eyeglasses perched low over his nose. He had been disturbed. It was late. Something was wrong. Xiao Li spoke to him, and the Russian's head swivelled slowly toward Newman like a gun emplacement. The eyes drew aim. The lips moved but Newman heard nothing, and then the Russian turned and closed the door, and Xiao Li shuffled back into Newman's apartment.

"He say he too busy."

"Sonofabitch!" whistled Newman.

He flew wildly through his music. Without a cello, it was all so effortless. Newman had to pull back several times because he discovered that he was not playing with the other two. And then later, when the Chinese walked down the hall and around the corner, and the *fuwuyuan*, having come out to enquire, went back into their little rooms, Newman stood and contemplated the door across from him. Again, no light from the door. Hadn't the Russian understood that he was to have been listening, that they had been playing for him?

The following night, someone knocked at Newman's door. He answered it and found Xiao Li there. Behind him, the Russian's door stood wide open, and in the middle of the room, two people, a young Chinese woman and the Russian. The Russian sat in a chair busily sawing his way through a piece of music.

Xiao Li said, "You come. He say."

"But where's Xiao Hu?"

"He go, look for Xiao Hui. You must come."

The Russian's snub gnawed away at him. "I mustn't do anything."

"He tell me ask you."

"No," said Newman, "I am too busy."

Newman exchanged glances with the Chinese girl studying him from the yellow light. She had a quizzical look on her pretty face, the appearance of one conducting an experiment whose hypothesis was about to be proven wrong.

"You know it. The Borodin."

"Borodin?"

"You have this."

"Oh, yes."

"You show me this."

"Yes, yes, I have the music."

The eyes of the girl reminded him of Janet Sellors, who often surveyed him from that very room. He took his violin, then, and crossed the hallway with Xiao Li. It felt strange entering Janet's apartment again, memories crowded in on him.

"This is Guo," said Xiao Li, "Guo Liyan."

"*Ni hao?*" he said, flexing.

"Hello," she said, dropping her eyes.

He sat in the circle and ran his bow across the strings of his violin. The Russian hadn't once looked up, hadn't acknowledged his presence in any way. Newman tuned to Guo, opened his musical part and stared at it. Somewhere beneath the odors of the Russian, he could smell the life of Janet Sellors, so brief a sojourn, so final its decree. There wasn't one thing of hers remaining in the room and yet it was as if she were everywhere. Newman looked back at Guo Liyan, and she looked at him, smiled the smile of a girl who knew that they lived in separate worlds with tall gates and fuwuyuan and long dark hallways between them, but after all was it so different from the distances between him and Janet Sellors?

They played too fast or too slow.

The cello of course set the tempi . . . and the mood. The Chinese were remarkably adaptable to these Russian tempi and moods, but Newman often found himself stranded and forgotten. He felt like a child at an adult's picnic. Once or twice he sought out the eyes of the girl, and she responded, now quickly and without comment, as if she knew he was there but so what? He went to find Xiao Li, but Xiao Li gave him his eyes in such a way as to say, you have your room, he has his, and right now we are in his room and he is telling me what to do, not you.

It seemed as if no one could remember that in a quartet it is the first violin that shows the way through the tempest. Yet the Russian hadn't looked once at him, and even when Newman turned to the Russian for guidance, nothing came of it. It was as if he had been brought into the music to fill up an empty chair.

"Why are you here?" Janet had asked.

"Why?" It seemed the thought had never occurred to him. "I don't know why. I just am. It's that time in my life."

"I am here because my whole life has driven me here."

"Don't tell them that," Newman said, cynically. He found refuge in cynicism. "They'll ask you to teach for nothing."

110

She hadn't heard him. "I don't mean China," she said. "This might as well be Chad. It doesn't matter where it is. You spend your whole life looking for something beyond you, something bigger, more important." She fingered a brass buddha and got a long look into her eyes. "Back home I couldn't find anything bigger than me . . . and I knew how small I was."

"I lost my job and someone told me they were looking for English teachers in China."

She ignored Newman. "The problem isn't here, the problem is what we bring with us. We expect . . . so much when we come and when we get here we find out it's just another place."

He said nothing, he wanted to hear her talk.

"This afternoon," she said, "I informed them I was leaving, and I gave them the names of people who had written to me to say they would be happy to fly themselves over here and finish out my contract." Her eyes were cloudy as she gazed into the autumnal leaving light. "They were cold, they said that since I had broken my contract, I'd have to find my own way home."

"But that's reasonable," said Newman, "I mean, well, after all, you did sign a contract—"

"You don't understand at all, do you!" she said. "This is something beyond contracts. You could call it . . . the death of the heart."

Newman played all the notes on the page just as an actor reads every word of the script the first time he sees it. He hadn't had a chance to put any feeling into it, because he was outside everyone else. He began to play for himself, and as they came down to the end of the first movement, he felt as if he were in some sort of a foot-race in which he clearly came in last.

He set his violin upon his knee and wiped the sweat from his face. The Russian flicked his eyes at Newman, but there was nothing written on them, and they all went about scanning the second movement. It was hot in the room, and all the windows were sealed and barred as if the Russian had built himself away from the world. Newman turned his eyes to the girl, and she looked at him. There was something in her eyes but he couldn't read it. A mystery, something about noncommitment, a divorce without a wedding. Let's forget it, she seemed to say, even before there was anything to forget.

The movement was 'Andante' but they played it 'Largo', and no matter what expression Newman gave, the Russian gave it more; and when he pulled back, the Russian vanished, so that, in the end, Newman stuck out like a sore elbow.

Janet had been able to pack everything into two huge, grey Samsonite suitcases and now looked pitifully small and left-over in the brown chair by the window. Newman drank the last of her imported scotch. At the far end of the room a young Chinese girl from Janet's institute sat fingering a *Time* and trying to follow their conversation. The last lights of autumn filled the room with their own sad farewells.

"Do you have everything?" he said. He looked at the two suitcases, and drank.

"I'm leaving everything." She looked as if she had dressed up for a funeral. "Are you sure you don't want any of this— " She pointed to the prints and the calligraphy. "— *dreck!*"

"No. It would only remind me of you." He tried to pack meaning into the words, but they sounded hollow. "Besides, the fu will certainly want them."

"Well, I don't want them, that's for sure," she sighed and got up, walked to the window. "I don't want anything to remind me of this place."

Newman finished his drink and went to stand behind her, noting how beautifully built she was. "Will you write?" he said. He placed one hand gingerly upon her shoulder and felt her stiffen.

"No," she said and placed one of her hands over his. "I'm a lousy letter writer."

"Me, too," he said, "but when I return . . ." It was too

112

strong; he pulled back and tried to rephrase it decently. "I've got your address, I'll look you up."

She turned and kissed him politely. "Yes," she said, "you do that, you look me up." He walked with her to her car, and when he returned, the *fu* were already dividing up the spoils. He thought for a moment to go inside, but when he saw the look on their faces as he approached the door, he stopped and smiled.

"*Duibuqi,*" he said. "I'm sorry."

"*Mei guanxi,*" they said.

And just like that it was all over.

The Russian won the second movement, and Newman got to his feet. He leaned graciously toward Xiao Guo, bowed and said, "*Zaijian,* sweetheart!" She smiled up at him as if she already knew what he was going to do before he did. "*Xie xie.*"

"Good-bye," she said, dropping her eyes.

He shook Xiao Li's hand and walked toward the door.

"Where are you going!" The words struck him in the back with all the force of a knife. Newman was so startled, he stumbled and swung about, wounded, and found the Russian staring hard at him. The eyes were hard and brittle, skyblue, they flashed unwaveringly.

"Home," said Newman.

"Home?" But we are not yet finished with this music!" The English was flawless. "You cannot go!"

Xiao Li and Xiao Guo flicked their heads back and forth as if watching a ping-pong match. It was always so difficult to understand what made the foreigners do the things they do and say the things they say.

"Cannot?"

"As I said, we have two more movements in this piece! You surely cannot simply walk out and leave the music hanging in mid-air!"

"Surely you do not mean 'cannot'?"

"I mean *cannot!*"

Newman spun about upon his heel and walked into the corridor while the Russian got up and followed him, shouting abuses in his own language. Newman stopped, turned to face him.

"Cannot, you say!" he shouted.

The *fuwuyuan,* dislodged from their small room, came out to look at them. Newman saw them, squared his shoulders and walked into his room, slamming the door behind him. He listened for a while, heard them trying to continue without him, the girl playing the first violin part. It was pitiful. Even the Russian foundered and fell, and then he heard the Chinese students leave, heard the door close, heard the long silence that followed in their wake. "Yes," Janet had said, "You look me up," but she hadn't meant it. He stared at the violin in his hand and saw his reflection in the mirror. He watched as he placed the violin to his shoulder, waited until he could find the tune he was looking for. It was the Borodin. It was there in his fingers, all of it, every note.

And he was well into it when he first heard the cello.

It caught him quite by surprise. He stopped and listened to the Russian, who had been playing along with him, note for note. He waited until he could find some place to enter, and when he did, he played low and light so that he could hear the Russian. Had the Russian actually heard Newman or was all this a mere accident?

Maybe it didn't matter at all. None of it, maybe nothing mattered at all.

THE PILGRIM

1

It would be an old dusty red bus. They'd make room for her up front so she would be the first to see it. Sages and scholars were there, and beautiful old waxy men wearing those thick round glasses and with skullcaps fitted real tight to their bronze domes, and they'd have these thin wispy white hairs sprouting out of their chins. They'd come and kneel in front of her and ask questions and she'd tell them how it all began the day she made a paper model of The Great Wall and then stood up in front of the fifth-grade class and described it to them. Oh, how they talked about her afterward! No, she'd say to them, I'm not a scholar, I'm just a common everyday housewife but I know more about The Great Wall than anybody else in Keokuk. I spent my whole life reading up on it. I know it's 10,000 *li* long and 26 feet high in some places, and I know the emperor Qin Shi Huang di started it in 221 B.C. Then the scholars would all smile at each other and the women would bring their children up to the front of the bus so she could lay her hands on top of their little heads and then at last when they drove up over that hill and saw it, oh my! it was just massive, more massive than anything she'd ever dreamed about as it snaked up over one mountain and down the next, one mountain after another until it turned purple and vanished from sight . . .

"*Qi!*"
What?
"*Qi chuang!*"

There it was again: that horrible nasty noise. She tried to step back into the shadows of her dream but someone was in the room walking around her bed and banging away at it and shouting at her in that foul and abusive babble. The purple mountains and the great rock wall faded and the red eye of morning fell upon her. She opened her eyes and saw one of *them* banging away at her bed. She wore a ridiculous white bag over her head and her very breath made you want to vomit.

"*Qi!*" she barked.

"What do you want, you miserable woman?"

"*Qi chuang.*"

"The least you could do is talk human!"

She tried to turn over and hide her head but of course she couldn't because they had her strapped to the bed. Here she was, 80 years old and strapped to her bed! Oh my beloved Jesus, even that time she told Harold to hell with it she'd take even more sleeping pills next time, they took her down to Keokuk Lutheran and, maybe they did put her to bed but at least they didn't strap her down, yet here she was, 80 years old and in a communist country and they had her down and strapped to a bed, deprived of every last vestige of her natural-born freedom. Her country had fought two world wars for her and still she didn't have a pot to piss in.

Not only that: during the night they had come and drugged her and God Himself only knew what they'd do to her today, probably take her out into the courtyard and shoot her in the back of the head just the way they do common criminals. Everything they said about communism was true! Well, she wasn't going to touch any of their food and she wasn't going to tell them anything. You just never knew what they were looking for. Still, you would have thought the American Embassy would try to protect you, but no, they sent you one of those smart-ass college women who was always talking about women's rights but then looked the other way when a real woman had her rights trampled on. They were probably all in cahoots. Ever since she got to China they had tried to strip away every last vestigate of her natural-born freedom. They had thrown her into a cell and then all trooped in to stare at her and when they saw she was properly strapped down, they went away again. Then she called out and one of them came and she told her she had to go to the toilet, and she was unstrapped and driven a long way down the hall to a horrible room and made to squat over a hole in the floor, and afterward she was driven back to her room and strapped down again. But she had seen all she needed to see: there were two doors to the toilet, and so the next time they took her down there, she'd sneak out the door and go out and hail a taxicab, and by the time they found her gone, she'd be halfway to the airport. She'd get on a plane and fly home, and then she'd call the newspaper and tell them how you were treated when you went to Peking. She flirted with the idea of getting the woman from the Embassy to help spring her, but when she heard her out in the hallway speaking in that awful language with the rest of them, she knew she was on her own. No, that American woman wouldn't spring her from the hospital, she only made a lot of promises she never kept, and when she got back to Keokuk, she'd tell the newspaper all about her, and there'd be an investigation and probably clean out the whole nest of them.

"Qi! Qi!"

The woman grabbed her arm but she pulled away. "Lemme go!" she screamed. "Get out of this room! You hear me? Get out of here!" She had to shout several times before the woman left her. Probably defective. Alone, she could plot her escape. She was sleepy, so sleepy. It was the drugs of course. They had given her drugs so when she slept they could come in and pry it out of her. It? What was it? She tried to think back over the past few days to the moment she stepped off the airplane but she kept slipping in and out like a door opening and closing. She tried to frame the letter she'd write the President. "Dear Mr. President," she'd say, "recently I returned from China, where I was subjected to the most inhumane treatment of my life. I was kidnapped and placed in a cell somewhere and they injected all kinds of drugs into me. But my chief complaint . . ." What was her chief complaint? "Your embassy staff was in cahoots . . ." Yes, that's what she'd say, in cahoots.

117

"Hello, Millie."

She pretended she was asleep. They had sent her that woman again. She was still trying to worm something out of her. She tried hard not to listen but unfortunately the woman was speaking English. You could close up to the abuse of that other noise, but English made it hard for her not to hear.

"Millie? It's me. Carol Cox. Remember me?" How could she forget, for Christ's sake? It was all part of the program to treat you like a child. That was how they did it all right. "I'm from the American Embassy. I was here to see you yesterday, remember?"

She cranked open one eye. "Let me ask you one question, Carol Cox," she said. "What do they want out of me?"

"Want?"

The broad was playing dumb. Fine, if that was the name of the game, she'd come across to her. "They got you strapped down to your bed, right?" She flicked open the other eye and for one moment she saw two of them out there, both ugly. "Every now and then they come in and shout at you and punch you around and then they bring you slop no human being could ever eat and then they push you down the hall to a toilet no human being could ever use. They call this a hospital? Since when is a hospital dark and dirty? Is this a hospital run by witch doctors or something? And why do they strap you into your bed like you're a crook? What do they want out of me?"

"That's more than one question, Millie." This one is just a beginner, she thought, otherwise she wouldn't play games. And of course using the first name was all part of the strategy. "They brought you to Central Hospital because you were found unconscious in a street near your hotel, and they figured you'd had a heart attack or a stroke."

So what do they expect when you come all this way just to see The Great Wall and all they showed you was a bunch of grey slums and people lined up from one end of the street to the next just to buy a couple carrots for supper, and the smell of vegetables just left to rot in the street like that, and no manners at all, everybody standing around gawking at you like you had a goiter or something.

"You wanna know why I was out in that street?" she said. The thing you had to do was confront them, tell them the truth because it always made them uncomfortable. "I got real thirsty when I checked into my room and I found a glass and took off the cellophane and held it under the faucet and ran myself a glass of water and I was just about to drink it when this room clerk just walked into my room without knocking and started to shout at me, and then he came over and grabbed the glass out of my hand and poured the water down the sink!" She watched the woman's face: it was made out of steel. She'd never show anything, that woman. "So I had to get out of that hotel. I went out into the street, it was so hot, but I couldn't go back inside, and I wandered around with my camera thinking I'd take some pictures to show them back home and . . . and . . ."

"You passed out."

"Wouldn't you?" No, she wouldn't. This was one of those people who spent all their time causing trouble at the university and then going out into the world to cause more. "I mean, I scraped every last penny I had together in one pile just to come over and see The Great Wall . . . I'm over eighty, you know. I ain't goin' to be around a whole lot longer. I got a right to see The Wall just like everybody else."

"What I'm trying to say—"

"I know what you're trying to say." She wasn't about to be pushed around by a woman whose salary she herself paid. "You think they've got a right to strap me down just because I was right in the first place when I told them to stop pushing me around and feeding me all that dope."

"Millie, I don't really think—"

"No, you don't think." She had to square this person away if she ever wanted to get out of China. "Just because you work at the Embassy don't mean you know everything. You ever been strapped to a bed in this joint? Huh? You wouldn't know how they treat you at night after everybody goes home." The Cox woman cowered, she adjusted her green eyes and crossed her arms. "Now you listen to me for a change. Maybe I did faint, so what? I'm old now, I'm way over eighty. I'm probably senile too, I don't know. I don't know and you don't know, so don't you go jump to any conclusions. Now, I got only one question and I want a proper answer. If I don't get it, I'm gonna have your ass in a sling as soon as I get back to Keokuk."

She had her right where she wanted her.

"I'm feeling pretty good right now, and still they got me strapped down to a bed. I came all this way, I spent my life's earnings just to get here. I came clear across the world just to see The Great Wall before I croak, and what I want to know is why they won't take this strap offa me and treat me like an ordinary everyday American citizen and why they can't give me a simple meal that ain't floating in a sea of grease!"

The woman at the side of the bed stared down at her own hands as if she just noticed they were dirty.

2

But it wasn't a bus and it wasn't red and instead of them having a busload of pilgrims in it, there was only one person in the automobile and it was one of *them.*

"You got to be kidding!" she said as they came out of the hospital and started toward the parking lot. She could feel her heart rattle about in its cage, and she smelled the garbage in the streets. However, she gathered herself and walked out into the stiff sunlight and stared at the car. "You expect me to climb into a car with one of them? You expect me to go all the way out there by myself?"

"I can't go along," said Carol Cox. There was a toughness in her voice that wasn't there yesterday. "I've seen the wall at least ten times already and besides I've got work to do."

"What am I paying taxes for? I paid taxes for over sixty years!" The woman didn't flinch a bit, she'd have to try something else. "You know I ain't got my two feet back on the ground yet. I can't go out there all the way by myself."

The door of the car opened, and a young Chinese girl climbed out and stood watching them approach.

120

"Anyi," said Carol Cox, happily, "this is Mrs. Markham. Millie Markham."

"How do you do, Mrs. Markham," said the girl. Okay, so she was pretty, so she had a pepsodent smile, so she wore American clothes. It was all part of the plan. She'd have to hijack the car and force them to drive her to the airport. "Miss Cox told me you came all the way to China just to see The Great Wall. It is a great privilege for me to take you there."

Likely story.

"Anyi is flying to the States in a few days to join her husband," said Carol Cox. "You've never seen The Wall, she's never seen The States. You two should have plenty to talk about." They literally shoved her into the backseat of the car and slammed the door on her. The Chinese girl climbed in beside her, and the Cox woman leaned through the open window. "Anyi and I will take you out to a restaurant when you come back. They serve the best steaks this side of Keokuk. And don't worry about your plane tickets, I've got you booked on a Pan Am flight to Chicago tomorrow afternoon. Maybe we can work it out so you and Anyi can fly back together . . . but we'll talk about that when you return. Have a nice day!"

The Cox woman got onto her bicycle just as they drove out of the lot, and she had to close her eyes because the driver took aim at a bunch of people in the road and then blasted them with his horn.

3

She sat way over on her side of the back seat and refused to talk. They weren't paying her to be sociable. She'd go out there and back because she didn't have any choice in the matter, but she wouldn't get out of the car and for sure she wouldn't look at The Great Wall. If that Cox woman was worth her salt, she'd have come along and earned the fat salary they paid her. She'd put all that into the letter. "That social worker at the Embassy was especially insulting," she'd say. "She shoved me into a car and forced me to go out there alone. I was very ill at the time but my repeated protests were ignored." Actually, she hadn't been feeling too bad ever since she talked her way out of the Funny Farm, but now, looking out the front window of the car, she knew she would probably get good and sick. So far as she could see there weren't any traffic rules in China, just bigger is better. Bicycles rode down pedestrians, cars rode down bicycles, trucks rode down cars. There were a billion people out there and they seemed all to want to use the road at the same time. Pigs and chickens, another billion, and carts and horses and police-men. Lots of policemen. Policemen everywhere. Most of them young, spanking-clean white uniforms, white gloves, red and gold badges, polished shoes. No guns, not one of them carrying a gun.

"That's funny."

"Pardon?"

What? Had she spoken out loud? The Chinese girl stared at her.

"I didn't say anything."

"I thought you said something."

"No, I didn't say anything."

"I heard you say something."

"I said your policemen don't even wear guns." She tried to make the words sound as if they were all that needed to be said on the subject. The girl had tried a couple times to strike up a conversation, but she had ignored her.

"No," she said.

"In America all the policemen have guns," she said, hating herself for saying it. "And they know how to use them too!" The girl was dressed like a university student all right, and she left her hair to grow out instead of tying it back into those awful pigtails like all the room clerks. Well, she did have a pretty face and what's more she didn't smell like the others. Still, she had to be wary of her. "You know," she said, sharpening her words on her teeth, "for someone going to the States, you sure don't know much." She fixed her eyes on the girl. "You say your husband is an American citizen?"

"Yes," she said, "he left a week ago for Springfield . . . Illi . . . Illionoise." She laughed at her own mistake. "He is a doctor and I am a nurse. But, you see, I want to study

122

medicine." She stopped and looked around for the words. "I know nothing about American customs; I am afraid I will be a big disappointment to him." The girl shook off her sadness and smiled again. "Is it nice in that part of your country . . . Springfield, Ill . . ?"

"I don't know, I live in Keokuk, Iowa. Folks where I live are honest and straight-forward. They don't strap you to a bed and feed you a bunch of slop." Still, she thought, there are a bunch of crooks around, too. "No, I wouldn't live anywhere else. It's the best country in the whole world. We don't have a whole lot of policemen standing around like you people do." Bite your tongue! she told herself. Anyway, it was a lie, there were lots of policemen in Keokuk and they all had guns and they carried them everywhere they went because *everybody else* had guns. And *they* were using them too. You just never knew when it was going to be your turn. Every night on TV they showed how some nut went into a store or a bank and just shot innocent everyday people down like a bunch of rats! Lots of break-ins too, rapes and muggings, things like that. Muriel Ansell for instance, sitting there that night just watching TV and knitting a sweater for her daughter Glynis, the one out in Denver, and in came that man and he had a gun and he made her strip right down in front of him, and she was sixty-seven years old. "I wouldn't live no place else, no siree!" She had to be strong now, maybe this was a test to see whether she had any weak points. "The best country in the whole wide world," she said, and of course it was, but still there were lots of things going bad now. Her husband, for instance. If his business hadn't gone belly-up, he'd still be alive today, she knew that. It was boom and bust, boom and bust, and he got way over his head in debt, and he went down to the bank and asked for an extension on his loan, and those bankers who had made money off him for twenty years or more wouldn't give it back to him and he came home and cried most of the night and not more than two months later he was dead. He went down like a lead sinker, they killed him, the bank and the loan officer, name of Snelling. She had gone down to Snelling's office to tell him that, but when she finally got around to the point she was trying to make, they pushed her out the door and told her to go home, but she didn't go home. She waited a little while and went back and stood outside Snelling's office and tried to talk to him, but someone came out and told her if she didn't go home, they'd call the police, and they did it too, and the police took her downtown and she . . . what happened then? Oh yeah, that was the first time she had her attack. They took her to the hospital and kept her for a couple weeks, and then she went home and found them walking around in her house stealing all of Harold's things. They wanted his car and all his tools, and she had to go to court, and that was the second time she got sick, went to the hospital, and the doctor put her on a strict diet. "No sir," she said, "I wouldn't live in China, it's just too . . . too . . ." She couldn't find the right word: she wanted to say 'overcrowded', but that wasn't it, and then she remembered the trip to Chicago to visit her daughter Alice and she took her to a big sale at Sears and she had never seen so many cars in one place in her life, and they had to walk a mile to get to a store jammed with people, and then after they bought the stuff and walked a mile back to the car, they started putting it into the trunk when they heard something breaking in front of the car and rushed out to find someone had thrown a brick through the windshield and Alice saw a bunch of Black kids and went to chase them and then she heard someone rummaging about in the trunk, turned and saw another Black boy running off with all the parcels they had just brought out of the store and she called for Alice but it was too late. The policeman wrote it all down in his little black book and told them there was nothing they could do about it because there were just too many cars and too many Black kids breaking into cars.

"And they had guns too," she said, "a whole lot of guns."

"Who?" The girl stared blankly at her.

"The police, of course. We had to go down to the police station and we went in and I saw so many guns in there I thought it was World War II all over again and then they told us there were over 500 people killed every year in that part of Chicago."

124

"You're not making it sound very nice," said the girl.

The pains were coming regularly now. She closed her eyes and remembered the words of Doc Morris, who had told her to think of something else just to take her mind off them.

"So how did you meet your husband if he's an American?"

The Chinese girl's story was long, and although she tried not to listen to it, she couldn't help herself because it was a real adventure story, and after a while she found she had become so absorbed in it that she had forgotten all about the pains in her arms and legs. It was a story of real courage and pain, not like Alice or Betty. Those girls had no backbone at all, just milksops. This was a story that reminded her of the romance of her own youth. She herself had had to fight for living space in a world made small by a bunch of old people who wore iron-hoop corsets and belly-length beards and preached "the old values", but she had gone out to Iowa to be on her own and to marry someone who knew how to cut down a tree without having it fall upon him. It had been tough in the beginning, especially during the Thirties, but she had come through it, even if her husband and daughters had turned soft.

There was something to the girl's story that a smart old whip like herself could see was not merely part of the brainwashing technique she had heard about. No, there was something hard and brilliant in the story that reminded her of the continent of her own life, and something long dormant in her rose up and went out to the girl. She almost felt like adopting her, maybe she had been wrong about her. Maybe they shared a world somewhere, maybe laws were laws and people were people. She felt a little dizzy, and once she thought she was going to faint, but she pulled herself through and even felt for a while as if she had conquered something weak in herself. Maybe it wasn't a red bus and maybe it wasn't loaded down with scholars and saints who gathered at her knees but then maybe this is the way the world is constructed, maybe it's not quite the way you think it is.

"I shouldn't even be here," she heard herself say. "I been sick a couple times already, and old Doc Morris, when

125

I told him where I was going, he tried to talk me out of it but, well, I'm pretty hardheaded and I get what I want when I want it." The girl seemed touched by her words. "You see, I've had a dream all these years. I figured just because I wrote a . . . silly little class report on The Great Wall, and Miss Hillyard made me repeat it for the PTA, and it made everybody back up for just one minute and look at me like I was kinda special, you know? I got the feeling somehow I really was kinda special. My daddy run a dry-goods store and he give me all his $1.98 specials to wear to school, but my mother, she kept me in braces until I was seventeen years old. I wasn't too popular, I can tell you. Then I made a fatal mistake: I married a stingy man who wouldn't take me nowhere. I didn't have much to do after that, so I had me two daughters, Alice and Betty, but all they ever did was drink beer and run around with boys, they never cracked a book and they couldn't care less when you told them The Great Wall was the only man-made thing on earth you could see from the moon." The girl sat and stared at her, and she felt the red line of pain opening up all the way from her shoulder down into her hip joint. She had pills for it in her purse, but now her purse seemed a million miles away. And she stopped talking to gather all her strength into her eyeballs because she knew she was almost there and she wanted to be ready. She fixed her eyes on the roadway curving up through the dry bushland as traffic began to pile up on itself. Like a snake, she drew herself down inside and prepared to strike.

"Thank you," said the girl.

It startled her. "For what?" she spat.

"For telling me all about America."

"I wasn't talking about America. I was talking about *me!*"

There was no time to talk now. They drove up into a sea of blue and yellow tourist buses and went around and around and around, swamped by thousands of fat and floppy breasts and navels sprouting with automatic cameras, T-shirts that said 'I Climbed The Great Wall' and motorbikes and taxicabs, all going round and round like water down a cesspool. At last they got mired down in a long line of cars going nowhere, and the driver snarled and turned to bark at the girl. They seemed miles from anywhere.

"He says we can get no closer," she said. "We'll have to get out and walk."

She climbed out into a furnace, and for a moment or so she was certain it was all over, she was going to expire here in the middle of chaos. She closed her eyes, better to see, but then suddenly she felt someone grasping her by the arm. It was her, the girl. "Come," Anyi said, "it's this way. It's not too far." Once she caught a glimpse of it, and it was *grand*, but not so grand as she had built it up in her mind over the past seventy years or so, but what came as a complete surprise and revelation to her was the strength and direction of the arm that moved her inexorably toward it.

"You're almost there," said the girl.

"Where?" she said, but the girl apparently was unable to hear her.

EXILE, EXULTATE

1

Play me a song of China, only make it modern. Soft, only a pipa or two, and then swell it into a grand opera with a cast of workers and how they overthrew the Guomindang and took sole possession of their own land for the first time since the Ming Dynasty, and then move andante into something more folksy, you know, with simple cowbells and gourds and flutes because you always end a song with something dark and sentimental about The People. And this is where I walk to stage centre and hand the old gateman Charles Langworthy's note.

He said, "*Bu zai.*" He folded the note carefully and handed it back. "*Tamen dou bu zai.*" He had only a tooth or so left but he showed them to me anyway as he sat down again on his short bamboo stool. "*Jintian wanshang laile.*"

I buttoned the note back into my pocket and walked past him into the compound. I heard him grumble and climb to his feet and shout, but I refused to stop. He started after me, but he was old and crippled and besides I knew he was wrong: the Langworthys were home and they were expecting me.

Inside the compound, the sandy courtyards were empty, and bare white fluorescent ceiling tubes blared from all the blank windows of the the the five-storey brick people boxes that walled them in from the streets. The buildings were all numbered in white paint; a maze of brick walls and tall thin windows and dark doorways, and in the open spaces only this flat plain of dirt swept clean early mornings by armies of little old women.

I found Doorway Number Three and walked up the dark, concrete staircase. Bicycles chained to the bannister tripped me up three times before I reached the fourth floor, where I felt my way to his door and knocked.

"Come in! Come in!" said Charles Langworthy. He was a short man, nearly bald, wrinkled, but with bright, flashing eyes. "You didn't have any trouble finding us?"

"As a matter of fact, I did," I said as he skinned the coat off me. "I showed your note to the gateman and he said you weren't in and you wouldn't be back until later. At least that's what I think he said. I left my Chinese at home."

"Did he try to stop you?"

"He came after me, but I was a little faster."

Charles Langworthy stared past me for a moment, and worry flags flew in his eyes. "I wonder who's there now? Maybe it's Lao Gao. I think he's been watching the gate this past week." He brightened and smiled. "Don't worry about it, I'll go down and talk to him."

Two women emerged from the back rooms of the flat.

"Hello, Elizabeth," I said.

"Hello, Marvin," she said. I had forgotten how beautiful Elizabeth Langworthy was. She dropped her beautiful eyes when I looked at her and placed her right hand on the arm of the woman standing beside her. "This is my mother, Dong Shaoli." I smiled to a small, exquisite Chinese woman who looked like an older version of Elizabeth. The girl had the features of her father, but they were established in the planes of her mother's face. "She speaks English, so be careful what you say."

"My English is very bad," said Dong Shaoli.

Langworthy ushered me past the women into a small room consisting of two beds, four wood chairs, a table with a silk cloth and platters of fresh pears, and in the corner, a desk. Bookshelves of Chinese and English books lined the three walls. The house was very Chinese, and in the white fluorescent light I could have sworn everyone in the room looked Chinese, even me.

"I hope you drink wine," he said, "because my wife brought home two bottles of French wine from the Friendship Store."

I sat in one of the chairs. "I drink to excess," I said and noticed that neither of the women had ventured into the room.

He poured two glasses of wine, handed me one and lifted his own to me. "Very well," he said, "here's to excess." I laughed at his little joke and tasted the wine. "Elizabeth tells me you play the tuba."

"I play at it."

"It's rather a strange instrument to take up."

"I didn't take it up," I said, hoping my private little joke would interest him. "It took me up."

I turned to look for Elizabeth, because she would have understood what I meant, but she wasn't there. The two women had gone to the kitchen.

"Yes, yes," he said, lighting a pipe, "it's the same with me. Things take me up. I'm an innocent, simple man, but I live in a world that seems designed to take up with innocent, simple men."

I lived in a hotel. But it wasn't a real hotel. It was a ghetto, a foreign ghetto where the "foreign experts" lived. It was a world unto itself, and it orbited around itself inside the walls of the hotel so that the Chinese people would be safe from its sinister influences.

Everyone at the hotel had heard of Charles Langworthy, but few saw him now because he avoided the hotel dining room, which was the Times Square of their lives. If he came to the hotel, it was for tennis or the Saturday night movies—Chinese films with English subtitles—not that Charles Langworthy needed subtitles because he had been living in China since 1937. Each autumn another herd of experts arrived at the hotel and were told about this *lao pengyou* who had come out to China in 1937 to cover the war for Reuters and had stayed through all the wars and civil bloodshed and natural and cultural disasters without returning home. A few of the *lao pengyou* lived at the hotel and had lived there since the Russians left it in a huff in 1960, and some lived at the universities (most of which were but a stone's throw from the hotel) and still others lived among the Chinese. Most of them came to the hotel for the tennis or the Saturday night movies or the Sunday dinner, the dances and all the other social events that took place in this foreign enclave.

But Langworthy had little to do with all this. Besides living somewhere deep in the *hutongs* and passageways of Old Beijing, it was said that he had married a Chinese woman just before the Cultural Revolution to save himself, and that their daughter Elizabeth, who was every bit as reclusive as her parents, was an employee at the *gong an*, the Chinese F.B.I. Perhaps it was this that attracted me to Charles Langworthy: the fact that he had escaped over to the other side and had a long story to tell, shards of which he flung at you from time to time when you got off alone with him. I often played tennis with Charles Langworthy for that reason. He ran about in his long johns and Mao cap, and as long as you hit the ball anywhere near him, he would hit it back to you.

The first time I met his wife and daughter was when he brought them to the movie theatre. We were going to be treated to "The General Without a Sword", a story about an officer who deserted the Guomindang. I sat next to Elizabeth and we talked quietly together for some time, and I asked her if it was true that she worked for the *gong an*. "No," she said, suppressing a laugh. "I work for an export and import company. I'm supposed to be a translator, but I spend every day at an empty desk reading old newspapers and drinking tea just like everybody else."

While we talked, her mother and father stared at the blank screen as if something was moving upon it. They whispered to one another from time to time. They seemed to have nothing at all in common with anybody else settled in behind the desks. During the day the room was a lecture hall, and on Saturday nights all the foreigners came to endure two hours of ideological thrills. Usually, the first film was a newsreel encomium. The wonders and blessings of the Four Modernizations! This was followed by a travelogue to one of the minority areas, where cute little girls in colorful costumes danced like fairies while the commentator pointed out how happy the minorities were to share in the Four Modernizations.

I told her I was a Canadian. Her mother tilted forward and looked over at me and smiled, "We want Elizabeth to go to university in Canada."

"I knew Bethune," said her father, nonchalantly. He bent over in front of his wife and spoke quietly. "I met him in a small town that had just been liberated by the Eighth Route Army. I asked him why he left Canada and he said there wasn't anything to do there."

"Times haven't changed," I said.

Even that first time, I found Charles Langworthy much more accessible than his daughter Elizabeth. I asked Elizabeth questions and he answered them. She was so beautiful. She struck me as a perfect expression of the two races, fusing her father's clear, powerful eyes with the sweetness and symmetry of her mother's round zen cheekbones. Elizabeth was small, delicate, defined, and she carried herself as if she were a rare piece of porcelain.

I invited them back to my rooms but they declined, saying the last bus left at 10:20; and so I walked them to the gate as Charles Langworthy spun an elaborate tale about the time he had visited the hotel during the Cultural Revolution and found all the foreign experts lined up in the road for a lecture about the Three Wrongs for Those Who are Both Red and Expert.

"Will you have more wine?" asked Charles Langworthy. I had to break loose from my memories. "I think we have time for one more teensy glass of wine before we eat."

"You know, Charles, I was just remembering the time you told me that story about going back to the hotel during the Cultural Revolution and finding all the experts lined up and being lectured. I never got around to asking you why they didn't line you up along with the rest of the foreign experts. Weren't you living at the hotel at that time?"

"No, that was shortly after I moved out of the hotel. I had just got married and because she was Chinese and already had a place to live and parents to look after, I had moved out." He dropped his voice. "They never lined me up for a lecture. They had better things to do with me." His smile vanished suddenly, and he stared at me with the eyes of a haunted man.

2

This is what he told me:

There were twenty or more who came for him that cold December morning. They roared into the yard in an old truck with a flatbed hung with red banners and *dazibao*— which characters he hastily translated as: "Beware of Foreign Friends who are Agents of the Imperialists" and "The Stinking Ninth Category".

And soon the stairway was full of them. They came running up the stairs and pounded on his door. He opened it and they told him he had to come with them at once, and that the woman had to remain behind in the apartment. They were all high-school kids, but for maybe one or two who were their teachers. Langworthy knew that they were going to take him out to the countryside and put him in solitary confinement. At least that was the rumour. And that Shaoli would be used as an example of what happens to Chinese people who marry foreigners. He put on his coat and kissed his wife. Nobody cried. His neighbours had come out of their apartments to watch. The Great Proletarian Cultural Revolution had come all too suddenly, too thoroughly, and nobody knew how far all this would go before Zhou Enlai could stop them and the government came to its senses.

He went down the steps with the soldiers. The courtyard was packed by the time he reached the ground floor, and when he emerged from the building, a great hush fell over the crowd. They walked him to the truck, and a pathway through the crowd was cleared by the Red Guards.

"Stinking Ninth Category!" someone shouted.
"Read and obey the Sayings of The Chairman!"
"Long Live World Revolution!"
"Make the foreigner pay!" shouted an old man.

Langworthy paused and stared at him. It was Lao Zhang, the shoemaker. "I have done nothing wrong, Old Zhang," he said. "I support the Central Committee and I hate the Four Olds. You know I have nothing Old in my house. I have faithfully served the Chinese people for thirty years now."

"You are a citizen of a hegemony."

"I am no such thing. I have a British passport."

"You have a British passport so you will take your wife and child back to Britain."

One of the Red Guards, a tall, handsome man, who kept his face immobile throughout, stepped in between them and said, "Imperialist fool, get up onto the truck!"

Langworthy surveyed the crowd and wanted to tell them they needn't be frightened by these juvenile delinquents, but, instead, he climbed up onto the flatbed of the truck and a half-dozen Guards surrounded him: one tied his hands behind him, another made him sit on a stool, and a third jammed a tall, white dunce's hat to his head; and, afterward, someone tied a red blindfold around his eyes. Langworthy hadn't had a chance to read what was written on it in *dazibao* but he imagined it said "Running Dog of the Imperialists" and "Foreigners are the Enemy of the People". Once seated, the rest of the Guards jumped up onto the flatbed and began to shout slogans at the crowd.

"Teachers are counter-revolutionists!" they cried. "The only correct knowledge is the knowledge of Chairman Mao! Read Chairman Mao and learn the Truth! Keep Party Discipline! Support the workers, peasants and soldiers!"

He waited for the stones, but after all, he was a foreigner and had to be treated with respect. Hated, but with respect. He held to the rungs of the stool as they pivoted through the streets, hearing from time to time, when the soldiers ran out of slogans, the sounds of the city— the buses, trucks, the bicycle bells, the chatter of children, the laughter and excitement. He loved the people of Beijing, he knew they were scared, he knew they were biding their time. He could tell that they stood and watched him as they whirled him through the streets, and he knew as well, though he could not see their faces, that most of them felt humiliated and frightened by what they saw.

In time the street sounds died out and the guards sang slogans with less conviction. They were going into the countryside, now climbing slowly, turning hairpins, the driver shifting into the lowest gear. They were taking him up into the Western Hills, where they would install him in one of the old Buddhist temples that snuggled in amongst the trees on the southern slope. He was cold by the time they paused before a gate which was swung open and closed again, and after a short drive, they stopped and the driver turned off the engine. Someone removed the blindfold, and, his hands still tied behind him, he was led across the the courtyard and beneath the elaborate blue tile roofs of the temple to a room in which an army officer rose to face him.

"Leave us, comrades!" he said, and the guards left the room, closing the door behind them. "My name is Wang," he said. The face expressed nothing. Every expression had been neutralized. "Please sit, Professor Langworthy," he said in English. "We sorry we do this."

"*Nin bu shuo Yingyu*," said Langworthy, "*wo hui Zhongwen.* You can speak Chinese to me. It is my native tongue. I live in China. The only time people speak English is when they want to practice. Do you want to practice your English?"

He ignored me and continued to speak English.

"You be here long time, Professor."

"What about my wife?"

"Nothing happen."

"What about me?"

"You stay here."

"Why? All the other foreign experts are allowed to remain with their families."

"I cannot answer."

"Why?"

"I cannot answer more."

The officer walked around to the door, opened it and shouted for a guard and told him to take Langworthy to his cell. It was dark and the way to the rear of the temple was by flashlight. He was shown into a small room without windows: it had a clean concrete floor, one bureau, a table, chair and a bed, and all this was presided over by a poster of the smiling Chairman. In time they brought him a lamp. Then one of the guards gave him a notebook and a pencil and a pencil sharpener. He wrote letters to his wife, and the guard took them into the office, where they were translated and sent to the *gong an* in Beijing. One day Officer Wang brought three English books and gave them to him: a grammar book, a collection of readings and Jack London's "White Fang".

"It is kind of you, comrade," said Langworthy.

"Do not mention it," said Wang. "Please do not show to soldiers. This is important."

The food was very bad—for breakfast, rice gruel with pickles and lukewarm tea, for lunch, a dish of rice and green things, and for supper, rice and green things and brown. He was allowed out of the cell only late at night, when he carried his slop pail to the toilet and emptied it into the ditch behind the toilet. He got sick shortly after he arrived and vomited all night, but nobody bothered to enquire into it. In the morning a guard came in and looked at him and then went and got a doctor. She came into the room and took his temperature, and when he spoke to her, she refused to respond. He tried two local dialects on her. She refused to look into his eyes. What he wanted to ask was whether there was any mail for him. When Officer Wang discovered he was ill, he sent to Beijing for a specialist, who came by nightfall and gave the prisoner a thorough examination and a bath. "You must take two of these pills every hour until you are well," he said. "It is because of the room. It is too cold in here. The food is not good. I will speak to Officer Wang." But Langworthy asked only about the mail. "Yes, yes," he said, "I shall ask about the mail."

Officer Wang came later that night and brought him a hot meal of bread, soup, chicken and rice, and a mooncake.

"A comrade bring mooncake from Wangfujing," he said.

"Have I received any mail?"

Wang shook his head.

"Didn't you send my letters?"

"Yes. But not worry, Professor. I know your wife fine."

"I want a letter."

Wang smiled. "You must come tonight," he said. "Bring books."

Later a guard opened his door and escorted him to Wang's office. Tea was brought in, the door closed and the officer smiled at him. "You will be re-educated. Rehabilitated." Langworthy sipped his tea. "I must teach you follow Chairman Mao. In English. But, first, you must teach me English," he said, smiling, nodding slowly. "My English very bad."

One month became two. Three became six. He heard nothing from his wife. He spent the long days of winter cooped up in his cold room, walking late afternoons unescorted across the courtyard between brick walls without seeing another soul, but for his guards, and then sitting in Wang's office for an hour or two, with hot tea and soup and chicken and pork, while Officer Wang tried to translate, word for word, the Works of Chairman Mao, and then, in the dark, the long, cold walk back to his cell.

"How long must I stay?" he asked Wang one day in spring, when the room was warm again. "And why can I not receive letters from my wife?"

"I try," said Wang. He was proud of his progress in English. "But, you see, local leaders, they say no. I cannot order them anything." He smiled and leaned closer. "Professor, you lucky. Some foreigners have all furniture removed. Some must work in field. Some die. You have food."

"What is happening in Beijing, comrade?"

"I bring you newspaper."

But there was no newspaper and no letter from home. In time, the little cell became quite comfortable. On the hottest day of summer a stove was installed but not connected until late in November, and then, with briquets, the room became very comfortable for the next winter. The food improved, and there was a variety of fresh vegetables and fruits. A toilet was dug near his door, and he was allowed to go to it whenever he wanted. The walls around his courtyard

137

were too high to see anything of the world, but he could hear traffic on the road and occasional shouting and laughter. Wang told him about the rallies in Tian'anmen and the speeches of Zhang Jing and the American war in Viet Nam.

The captor and the captive became friends, and Wang taught Langworthy calligraphy so that he would be able to write the Works of Chairman Mao in Chinese. Meanwhile his English improved to the point where he was beginning to write long passages about Norman Bethune and the heroes of the Revolution in the English language. Both were discovering each other through their study of each other's language.

One dark night during the third spring of his captivity, there was a knock at his door. Langworthy was a light sleeper; he sat up on his bed and called out. The door was opened, and Wang came in bearing a lamp. "Comrade Professor, I have brought you a guest," he said and went back to the door, reached across the darkness and took the hand of a person who stood in the courtyard.

It was Dong Shaoli.

Langworthy uttered a cry and leaped from the bed, rushed across the cold floor in his nightshirt and embraced her. The tears broke from his eyes. He stood for some time without looking at her, holding her close, feeling her soft body, and then he kissed her. She stood inflexible, cold, hard. Langworthy looked toward Wang. The officer stood in the shadows smiling, but he had tears in his eyes.

"She will stay until morning," he said. "But we must take her back to Beijing before light."

Once Officer Wang was gone, she relaxed and began to smile. It was a short night. They talked and talked. Dong Shaoli was now working in a hospital, cleaning latrines and hauling sour vegetables in a small cart out into the countryside. She was, however, physically well. She talked about the events in the capitol, the shootings and the parades and the problems with food, but she really knew less about the country as a whole than he.

"Tell me about Beijing," he said.

"Lin Biao is in charge. People everywhere are in jail."

"Are your neighbours hard on you?"

"Only when someone is watching. When everyone is gone, they bring me food and coal. I am well."

"But what about the other foreigners?"

"They are fine."

"All the families are together?"

"All but one or two. This will all be over shortly, people say. Just stay out of trouble. Do what they tell you to do. Don't make any trouble. People listen to Zhou En Lai. They hope. It will soon be over and you can come back home."

"Why are they detaining me?"

"I do not know."

They stopped talking toward morning and climbed into his bed. Nine months later Elizabeth was born.

3

Braised eggplant, gluten balls, stewed five-flavour beef, four precious vegetables, shredded beef with onions, steamed black carp, diced curried chicken, precious pork, fish ball soup and Hangzhou mooncakes.

The women brought the plates one by one out of the kitchen and then wooden chairs and sat without a word across from us.

"Your father was telling me about the Cultural Revolution," said Hagstrom, looking at Elizabeth. He had, after all, come to see her. "It was a difficult time for all of you."

"Yes," is all she said.

"My husband likes to tell stories," said Dong Shaoli. "It is nice to see he has someone to tell them to."

It was a small, dark house. It was made of crude concrete blocks, badly stapled together and leaking wind. The windows had been made in a factory that made windows that were supposed to fit anywhere. The only light in the room was a four-feet tube of white fluorescence whose white base was rusty and fallen at one end. A copper intestine of electrical wires could be seen coiled up inside the hole in the concrete. Yet the Langworthys had somehow learned to live in it; not only live in it, but to go with it, become one with it, to live without anything, to put up with the world the way it was constructed.

Hagstrom tried on several occasions to talk to Elizabeth, but the girl only smiled at him and answered his queries in a way that required her father to conclude her sentences. It didn't seem as if she had been coerced or threatened to do anything, and yet she did them. And when the meal was over, the women carried everything out with them, and Hagstrom decided it was time for him to get back to the hotel. He used the same argument they used on him: that, of course, the last bus was in twenty minutes, and so he had to return.

Elizabeth came to the door to help her father put on his jacket. Langworthy wanted to go have a word with the gateman. Hagstrom smiled at Elizabeth, helplessly, and then turned to walk down the stairs in the dark and to fight his way through the bicycles to the yard. At the gate Langworthy held a long loud talk with the old man, and at last, Hagstrom had to shake hands with the gateman and to exchange the few nickles and dimes of Chinese that he had in his possession.

They walked down the dimly-lit street together.

It was a typical street in Beijing: grey brick houses shouldered into one another along the narrow causeway, punctuated with slate-roofed, ancient doorways and crude, wood gates locked against the world, and in between the steep-roofed houses, the twelve-foot walls, also grey brick. In fact, it was a grey brick world, but the bricks had been plastered over for five hundred years, and where the plaster had fallen, they had been replastered and replastered, so that in any one place, you could read the history of the human race in the tones of plaster and paint.

"I was very interested in your story," I said, as we walked in the gloom. "How did you escape?"

He snorted to himself and looked at me. "It took me three years to figure out that Officer Wang was keeping me locked up because he wanted to speak perfect English. It wasn't enough for him to mouth it, say the right things. He wanted to speak English like a native. He wanted to be on top when the Cultural Revolution was over and he could get a job as a translator or maybe work in an embassy. I was the only foreigner there. I figured he didn't want anybody to know that I was still there because they'd come and get me and then his English education was up. I went to him one night and told him as much. He got angry and locked me up for a week. I didn't see anybody for a week. The food was shoved under the door. At the end of the week he had me brought to his office, and he apologized profusely and told me I was going to be taken to Beijing. He stood up and shook my hands and walked from the room. I was led into another room where they gave me new clothes and a good wash and then they took me out to a truck and drove me toward the city. They took me to a rehabilitation camp in the suburbs of Beijing. I knew the place. It had been an army band barracks. They led me up to a room, and inside it was Dong Shaoli. She had carried everything we owned out of our old apartment and brought it to our new house. She took me into another room and I saw for the very first time, my own daughter."

"Elizabeth?"

"Yes."

"What about Officer Wang?"

"Come with me," he laughed, pulling me into a narrow lane. "I want to show you something."

The streetlamps were few and far between. The lane wound its way between the walls until it came to a tall gate whose twin pillars had been crudely painted red with huge white lettering on it, which they call *dazibao*, and between the patched archways, the wooden door, warped and repainted a million times. We paused and I stared into the courtyard: some crude granite steps had been piled up to a doorway, weathered and white, the windows chinked into the openings, a rusted stovepipe at an absurd angle, a cane pram before the steps, painted red and yellow, the eaves of the building sagging but properly stopped with round ceramic tile adornments, each one with an emblem of the Qing in it.

We stood there for a moment or so before Langworthy leaned toward me, but just as he was about to speak, the door opened and an old man tottered down the steps and came toward us, stepping gingerly over the wooden doorframe. It wasn't until he came down the steps that he saw us and he quickly smiled and raised his hands and began to speak.

Langworthy hugged him and the two of them talked for some time, and then they turned to me.

"This is a friend from Canada," said Langworthy in English. "He has been visiting me."

"I am very pleased to meet you," said the Chinese man, a broad grin washing across his beautiful parchment face. "I am honoured that Mr. Langworthy has brought you to our little neighborhood. Well, from Canada! The land of Dr. Bethune."

"Yes, thank you," I said.

They spoke to each other again in Chinese for a while, and then Langworthy turned to me again. "I am afraid we must hurry," he said. "The last bus goes any moment now."

"Yes, well," said the Chinese man, "I hope you will return to visit us some day."

We continued along the lane until we reached the high lamp post that carried the number of the bus I was to take. Charles Langworthy leaned close to me at that point and said, "That, Hagstrom, was Officer Wang," said Langworthy. "You know, I haven't seen him in a while. He doesn't look very good, does he? Oh, we've become good friends, you know. I've been to his house many times, and Shaoli and I have had him and his wife over. You see, I learned much later that Officer Wang made sure that Shaoli was not injured while I was locked up in his little domain. Yes, he took care of her. Made sure nothing happened to her while I was away."

We stood for a while waiting for the bus. We seemed to have run out of conversation, and then, seeing the bus coming, I thought it was time to say what was on my mind, and I said it.

"By the way," I said, smiling, holding out my hand, "I want to thank you for having me to your home."

"Think nothing of it."

"I would have liked to hear more from Elizabeth."

"Yes," he laughed. "I always do that, you know. Men come to visit Elizabeth, and I find that I'm the one who has to entertain them." He found that very funny and spent a great deal of time laughing at it. He noticed that I wasn't able to share the fun. "Oh, listen, I'm really sorry about all this really. I have had a good time. How about tennis? Next Monday. I know it's cold, but if you run a little, you don't notice it."

"Mr. Langworthy," I said, "why won't Elizabeth talk to me?"

He suddenly frowned. "I thought she talked to you the other night at the movies."

"She invited me to your house."

"I know that."

"But she spent the whole evening out in the kitchen."

"Look," he said, suddenly, confessing, "I wouldn't let this get in the way of a game of tennis but . . . well, you see, Elizabeth is already quite serious about a young man who works in her office. I'm afraid she doesn't show much interest in *waiguoren* anymore. She's had her chances. She says she doesn't want to live overseas." He looked deeply into my eyes. "Oh, look, don't take this personally."

There was something about the way he pronounced *waiguoren* that said everything he wanted to tell me.

ZAIJIAN, NORMA JAMES

Norma James watched the *fuwuyuan* from her window. They rose without getting up and walked away standing still. They finished their sweeping but the yard was unswept. They gathered together in the shade leaning against their brooms and laughed as if they hadn't a care in the world, as if what they had done and were about to do had nothing to do with them, as if nothing really mattered.

They had only one small cupboard in this world and lived in a society in which others had no more, no less. Society took care of them from the dawn of their lives to the last black hour, and they understood too that the only thing expected in return was obedience and selfless devotion to just such meaningless tasks. So they rose early and laboured for two hours in their tomblike rooms and then came to work, where they rested. At midday they lay down for a two-hour *xiuxi* and after rising to an afternoon of make-work, which they accomplished with quiet and deliberate motions, they went home and spent long hours slaving over tiny gas stoves and washing and bathing out of pails and then going to bed early in cold apartments with long dark stairwells full of bicycles tethered to the railings.

They began at last to disperse, trailing their brooms through the dust toward their closets, where they would drink green tea and read yesterday's papers until it was time to begin cleaning the rooms of the foreigners. Most of the foreigners would be at work by then and so they could take their time and page through *Time* and *Macleans* and look unashamedly at the portrait of an outside world where gay

144

things happened to rich, well-dressed people . . . or they might switch on the foreigner's ghetto-blaster and listen to Talking Heads or Paul Simon. They had lots of time. On their way back down the steps, they'd drag their DDT-laden mops to their little dark rooms.

And so it went seven days a week, three hundred and sixty- five days a year— till they were fifty years old and then they went home for good and took care of grand-children and watched television. There was of course much to be said for all this.

Much. Much to be said for it.

The sun sat high in the dry rustle of birch trees resonating with the hysterical cries of the cicadas, and the earth smelled hot. A black and white thatch bird with a long tail flew into the leaves and silence reigned until it left again. A red canopy of dust hung in the sky above Haidian, and the Western Hills looked like a reclining dragon upon the vague horizon. Norma waited until she heard one of the *fuwuyuan* place a bottle of boiled water at her door and then she went out to fetch it.

"*Ni zao!*" said the girl. Xiao Liu. The pleasant one who had often tried to make Norma feel at home in this strange land. "*Hen hao de!*" she said, pointing to the new housecoat Norma had purchased at a small silk shop outside the north wall of the Temple of Heaven.

"*Ni zao, Xiao Liu! Xie xie!*" Norma said, bowing. There wasn't much more communication possible since the girl couldn't speak English and Norma's Chinese consisted of hello and goodbye.

She closed the door and made herself a cup of tea. She was a coffee addict, but in China good coffee was hard to find, and so she had submitted to tea. She went back into her long and narrow sitting room and looked at the letter. It lay where she had left it, on the small round glass table. She hoped in time it would become part of the debris and even disappear. The letter was from Frank. She had read it only once. She knew ahead of time what it would say, and when she had finished it, she carefully laid it back inside the envelope. The iridescent words flashed at her like the dial of a clock when she closed her eyes, and only by getting up and walking the planks in the dark could she avoid looking at the neon words, and then toward morning, when she tried to sleep again, she saw them in her dreams: they pointed fingers at her and counted off the days she had left in China.

Okay, she would return to Vancouver. Sure, Frank could play husband for a day and meet at the airport and drive her to her apartment in the West End and then go out to Momma James's, where he lived. Yes, she would look after her son Danny. She would search for a job. Of course she would fix the Saturday night dinner as usual, while Danny and his father sat and drank beer and watched hockey mayhem as if for two hours they could even bear the thought that they were related. Of course she'd go out to Mamma James's for the Bible readings and sit and watch the Sunday afternoon rains wash the mountains away. She would sit with Frank in the car on the long, lonely drive back to the West End and wait for him to make the first move, and when, as usual, he failed, she would get out of the car and walk to the elevator and spend the evening all by herself.

She could handle all that. Even if, as he had once said, he would have to get a divorce. She could go through all that. In November, Danny would be 18, and then he wouldn't be a problem for either one of them. She would ask the boy to move out, and if he didn't, she'd make it difficult for him and then he'd move out. No, it wasn't Frank. It wasn't the letter that bothered her.

It was the going home.

Home.

Where you got up in the morning rain and had to worry about leaving your apartment and walking down the deserted hallway to the elevator and climbing into the empty elevator and disembarking into the dark underground garage. You had to worry about sitting in an old rusty tub of bolts that had to be driven up the long corrugated ramp and out into narrow busy streets and down a long tunnel of red lights, and when you stopped for one of them, they piled into you and you got whiplash. No, you knew nothing about automobiles and you didn't want to know. So you took it to a service station and stood around in the cold uncomfortable waiting room while, for $40 an hour, greasy boys probed about in the belly of the old Austin and came back to you with the look of physicians who had bad news. Or it was trying to find some place to put the automobile, circling the lot, crowding into a small space by scratching the entire length of cars on both sides of you, and walking through the parking lot where thugs lurked and finding your way into the market where they played tricks on you by hiding the food you wanted and positioning junk at eye-level, making the price of everything secret. It was full of chemicals anyway, and so you had to drive around town looking for a health food store where everything was in barrels so you didn't know you were paying three times as much for it as you paid for the chemicals.

Her telephone snarled. It was the low, thrilling voice of Martha Patten, who reminded her about the banquet. Norma told her she had decided not to go.

"You don't have a say in the matter," said Martha. "You have to go."

"Well, I'm not going and that's all there is to it!"

"Norma, this is China."

"Don't rub it in."

"This is your farewell banquet. You do what they tell you to do."

Norma resolved her voice into the minor. "You don't understand anything, do you? I simply cannot go."

"Cannot?"

"No, I can't."

"Why can't you?"

"Because."

"Are you sick?"

"Yes."

There was a long pause. She heard the *fuwuyuan* in the hallway. They were laughing at something and shouting down the stairwell.

"Norma, what's going on? Last night you looked like death warmed up. If it has to do with going home again—"

She had struck a nerve and Norma jumped. "It has

147

nothing to do with that."

Martha spoke as if the words hurt her mouth. "Something's going on. Why won't you talk about it?"

"Nothing's going on!" she screamed. Too late to recall the words. "Nothing, nothing. Nothing's the matter."

"I'm coming over— "

"No!

"I'll be right there."

Norma slammed the telephone together. "Bitch!" she said to herself, walking to the window, brushing back her tears. She had to get out of there. She had to escape. She quickly dressed in her blue running suit and put on her shoes, ran to the peg beside the door and slipped off her bicycle key. She locked the door and ran past the *fuwuyuan* gathered along the steps reading from a comic book one of them had found in a wastebasket. Martha would probably take the elevator, and so Norma ran down the stairs and out into the lobby, flicked the fly-bead curtain aside. She looked quickly toward Building 9, where Martha lived, and crossed the road to her bicycle, which was parked below the birch trees, and after fumbling with the lock, mounted and sped along the curving road that led out to the hotel gate, where she dismounted and walked her bike, as was the custom, and then mounted it again and rode south into the traffic along Baishiqiaolu, the Road of the White Stone Bridge.

God, it felt good to be free again! It felt good to be part of the flowing blue river of bicycles pouring down the hill beneath the towering birch trees and past the rising concrete shell of the national archives, where one day they would lay to rest the national soul. She was pleased that they had preserved the magic roof and lofty rigid geometry of the ancient Ming temples.

She was proud of herself, pleased with the way she navigated among the Chinese. She felt, curiously, a part of the world when she rode her bicycle among them. She made all the right moves. They had to look twice before they realized she was a foreigner. She shared a common language with them— the bicycle. Together, then, they moved past the waterfall of flowers at the gate of Purple Bamboo Park and through the tall shadow of the new Xiyuan Hotel and into the ordered chaos of the the zoo and around the tall Soviet nail of the Exhibition Grounds and up the ramp and into the tangle of the cloverleaf above the Second Ring Road, where now only a few cars snored along the wide concrete runways.

The thing about Zhou Pei Ling, he was damn good-looking. It had taken a while for her to appreciate Chinese men because, well, because at first she thought they all looked alike. Zhou was different. He was quintessentially Han—tall, proud, piercing eyes, buddhist cheek bones, an honest mouth. In time she came to appreciate Chinese men because, unlike Westerners, they never seemed to threaten, never seemed stung by machismo or the need to prove something. They were, of course, curiously non-personal in their dealings with women, and although often they walked with their arms around other men, they seemed never to want to touch a woman. Sexual needs never seemed to burn about their eyes, and yet at the same time she discerned something like a rare passive kind of sensuality and the promise of smouldering desire.

Zhou Pei Ling—

"Call me 'Joe'," he said the day they met. "Joe Bailey. That is the name they gave me when I was a student in London."

"I can't," she said. "It's too familiar. We don't know each other."

He laughed nervously. "Perhaps, then, in time."

"Yes," she said, soberly, "perhaps."

Zhou Pei Ling was chairman of the foreign languages department, and as such took her under his wing and showed her the university. They never showed foreigners the university grounds behind the new classroom building. It was frankly a half-hearted attempt to convert an old movie lot into a modern university: the sound stages were gymnasiums, the previewing rooms offices, and behind the coal heaps, the student dormitories and dining rooms. It was here that Norma finally realized she was teaching in the Third World. Still, the students were enthusiastic and the faculty clever and long-suffering, and, in short, she dove into her work like a fish long out of water, and by the time spring arrived, she was in love with her new university.

It was April, and Zhou had invited her to see a movie on Norman Bethune. She went along with him to a brand-new theatre and as she entered the cold room, students and faculty already there turned and applauded as she entered. Zhou got up and gave a speech about Dr. Bethune and talked about the friendship between Canada and China and about the dedication and excellence of the Canadian teacher in their midst, and after another round of sincere applause, the lights went out and they watched a frankly romantic portrait of the man who invented M.A.S.H. and revolutionized medical practice.

And afterward Zhou walked her out to the front gate, where her taxi waited. "When I am a boy," he said, "I imagine Dr. Bethune is a god. I think he come from heaven." He laughed to himself. "I think Canada is heaven and Canadian mountains are modern Mount Olympus."

"Canada has mountains," she said, "but I'm afraid we don't have any gods living there just now."

"And I hope I can go to mountains," he continued, as if he hadn't heard her. "But, you see, they send me to London for my master's degree." They walked quietly for a moment and then he turned to her. "Now, it seems, I have a chance. You see, I have been told by my government I may go to Canada to study."

"That's wonderful, Zhou!"

"Thank you, thank you," he said. They walked through the gate, and he opened the car door for her. She slid into the back seat and was surprised to see him leaning in and leering at her. "Norma," he said. "I hope . . . you will help me."

"Of course," she said.

"You see, I have no money to study. I must receive a scholarship or perhaps a job at university."

After the cab pulled out into the narrow road, she turned and looked back toward the gate. He stood there waving to her and smiling.

Students and teachers alike ran for the dining room early as if they expected to find there was not enough food to go around. Zhou, however, was always the last man out of his office, and when Norma heard him making his moves, she went and knocked at his open door.

"Can we talk?" she asked. He smiled as she took a seat in front of his desk. He sat down and frowned at her. "Zhou, I don't want to go back to Canada. I want to stay here for another year." He stared at the floor as if looking for a trapdoor. "I don't want to go back to my little cell in Vancouver and sit around by the telephone all day waiting for them to call me just because somehow they found some money in a discretionary fund and now they can offer me a job for a couple months at minimum wage. I don't want to take a job and hang around faculty rooms looking like a wet dog somebody hauled ashore." He was, frankly, embarrassed and perhaps even a little insulted by her confession. "There's nothing for me to do in Canada. Don't you see, Zhou, I'm a refugee. I want to claim refugee status. You signed the Helsinki accords, didn't you? You can't send me home."

He laughed quickly in embarrassment. "I'm very sorry," he said, "very sorry." He sat up and faced her. "You see, we have already hired another, um, professor."

"Unhire her then."

A laugh. "I'm afraid that would be impossible—"

"Okay," she said, hardening, "you remember you asked me three months ago to help you find a job in Canada?"

"Yes," he said. "I understand. You cannot help me. You have explained this—"

"Well, I change my mind." She stared at him before she said it, and when she said it, she launched the words at him. "You want to go to Canada, right?" He studied her. "I want to stay in China, right?" He didn't like it: it reeked of subversion. "Okay, I'll get you into a Canadian university if you keep me here for another year."

He flicked his eyes about the room as if searching for microphones and said, "I'm very sorry, I cannot help you. The problem is Vice-president Li writes letter and the professor returns contract. Everything down in black and white."

She scarcely knew she had said the words until she heard them coming as if from a long way off and they came so fast and furious that she could only flinch as they stung the back of her teeth and forced her mouth to fly. "I've been in your country long enough to understand the way things work," she said, "and the way things work here is if you want something from somebody else, you can get it only if you're prepared to give something back in return . . ."

The tears came to her eyes and she felt faint. She got to her feet somehow and stumbled out of the room.

Hers was a Flying Pigeon.

She loved her Flying Pigeon. It steadied her as it flew her silently and efficiently through the chaos of Beijing's roads and supported her in the brick maze of the *hutongs*, where narrow, winding lanes went everywhere and nowhere. She had mastered the science of flight, she was so perfect in motion, so graceful as she manoeuvered on silver spokes along the finger lakes the Empress Dowager had travelled on her weekly sailings from the Forbidden City to the Summer Palace. She slipped past the high purple walls of Madame Soong's residence and down into Beihai Park and the Jade Bowl, where once Kublai Khan had dwelt, and the great white Dagoba, the centrepiece of Xanadu, which in the bright July sun looked like an ancient space-ship about to launch. She came out at Coal Hill, crowned with temples and trees, one still wearing the collar from which the last Ming emperor hanged himself.

Her Flying Pigeon was blue, like a Beijing December sky. Youmei had called it 'Homing Pigeon' by mistake the first time he saw it. They laughed together . . . God, how they had laughed! It was blue, very blue, she discovered. It stuck out among all the black ones. Blue like a Beijing December sky, as they rode together. Youmei was not particularly handsome, but he was witty and good-natured. "*Fenghuang*," he had said. "We translate that as . . . 'Homing Pigeon'." And they had laughed. They rode together in through the hole in the south wall of the Summer Palace and spent the day alone together, sitting among the rushes and talking about China,

152

what it all meant, how it worked, what he wanted, what he feared. Her bicycle was so blue that they had to hide it when she went to visit him at his apartment block.

"Yes," she said, "it is like a homing pigeon. It flew me straight to your house."

She rode her blue Flying Pigeon around the Forbidden City and south toward the Peking Hotel and thought about Youmei. Youmei had a gentle, round, warm face. He had large eyes which he disguised with issue plastic-rimmed spectacles, and he always wore a Mao cap drawn tight about his ears. "For protection," he used to say. And he had one of those perfect Chinese noses and a perfect smile. She had turned away from him that day they met and studied the scene in the doorway of the bus. The young female conductor was arguing with people sandwiched in the doorway, saying the bus wouldn't pull out until they got off. But they weren't getting off for anyone. The driver of the bus examined them in the rear-view mirror and decided there was little he could do but to turn off the motor and save fuel.

And when she turned to look at him again, he said, "You speak English?"

"Yes," she said, looking away.

"You are teacher?"

"Yes."

He was undeterred. "You teach at university?"

She turned to look at him again. "The Banking Institute."

"You are banker?"

"No." She smiled. "I teach English to banking students."

He smiled. The bus sat there and nobody said a word; the people in the doorway refused to look guilty.

"How old are you?" he said, suddenly.

She fixed her eyes upon him. "That is impolite."

He scanned his thesaurus, but he couldn't find the word.

"How old do you think?" she said.

153

"I cannot tell. Thirty years old."

She laughed out loud. Other people looked at her. "How old are you?" she said.

"Thirty-eight years old."

"I am ten years older than you."

He expressed no surprise, leaning a little closer to her. "Do you like China?"

"Oh, yes!" she said.

"Where do you live? At the Youyi Binguan?" She nodded. "Are you married?"

"You ask a lot of questions."

He merely stared at her.

"I am married but I do not live with my husband. I have not lived with my husband for ten years or more. We merely tolerate one another from a distance."

He said nothing.

"Don't ask me any more questions."

Suddenly the door closed and the bus lumbered out into traffic. The passengers were silent as if the forward motion of the bus was not to be complicated with speech, but when they reached the corner before the giant gymnasium, he was talking again.

"I not ask questions."

"Don't even speak," she said, staring. She had not prepared herself for this, and even as the man spoke to her, she could feel something like heat coming from him. The odor of his body frightened her, but not as much as the unflinching eyes which seemed to be seeing things in her that she wanted hidden. They stared at each other for some time without saying anything, and then she realized that she had gone straight past the hotel.

"Yes," he said, as if he understood her nervousness, "I want to speak . . . but you say—"

"Goddamn it!" she said and tried to force her way through the great wall of bodies between her and the door. It had to be something akin to driving one's flesh through the front line of the Montreal Canadiens. And once out in the street, she pulled herself together and realized he was standing beside her. She took a few tentative steps onto the sidewalk and realized she didn't have any idea where she was.

"In this direction," he said to her, pointing with his gloved hand. "The hotel is not too far away." She ought to have walked away; she ought to have done what she knew she was supposed to do. Why had she stood there like a school-girl while he talked openly to her. "You see," he began, "my flat . . . it is very near to here. It is in this direction, too. You will come. We will drink tea. You like tea? It is close. We will walk."

The two of them walked through the crude brick gateway and into the muddy yard that lay between two giant concrete apartment houses. He walked like a guilty boy past an old woman who stared at Norma as if she were a wild animal, and the old man sitting on the bench spoke to them. She couldn't understand the words and was surprised to watch the frightened look that had come into his eyes. They continued along a path that led around the puddles and arrived at the cement steps of the apartment. He spoke angrily to the woman who ran the elevator up to the twelfth floor, and while they walked along the cold dark hallway he ignored her. At the far end he took out a key and opened the door, standing just outside it with a grey face.

She walked into the apartment and stood quietly as he closed, and locked, the door.

"Now, will you drink tea?" The light tone of his voice made her turn. He was smiling openly now and he came to her. He came too close. It wasn't like a Chinese man to come so close. She could smell the garlic. "I will make some tea."

"Thank you," she said.

"It will cost you too little," he said, wrinkling his eyes. "You must teach me English."

That was it. She had been kidnapped by a man who wanted her jewels: the English language.

Norma rolled through the plaza before the high red gate where the emperor used to come to deliver his speeches and dispatch the heads of the enemies of the state. She turned

155

and rode through the crowd of visitors pouring into their 'forbidden city', diving into the long tunnel, and up over the middle of the five arched bridges. She had come to Tian'anmen.

"May I call you 'Norman'?" he asked.

"Norma," she said. "My name is 'Norma'. 'Norman' is a man's name."

"Yes. I shall call you 'Norma'."

"And what shall I call you?"

"You may call me 'Youmei'."

"Youmei."

It was much brighter in the square than anywhere else in the ancient city. She stood spread-eagled above her *fenghuang* and looked out to the obelisk at the centre. She felt eyes on the back of her head, turned and peered straight up into the eyes of the Chairman. Yes, they were kind, they had an avuncular sheen, it was a mystic's smile. But the painter had taken it all much too seriously. Mao was too high above the world. He looked too far off. He appeared to see nothing. She rode down into the square and around the monument to the heroes of the Revolution and up to the tomb of the Chairman Himself.

"Are you married, Youmei?"

"Yes." There wasn't a moment's hesitation as he poured the tea into the cups. "I married and have two child."

"Children."

"Ah, yes! My English so poor. You must teach me English."

"Why? Why is it so important? It is just a language. Don't take it so seriously."

He was, however, very serious. "If you speak English," he said thoughtfully, "you can speak to . . . foreigners like you."

It was meant playfully, but there was another voice

inside this one and it was talking at the same time. After a while she listened to that one and compared it to the public one.

"Why should you meet foreigners like me? We are very . . . dangerous. They must have told you that."

"Yes," he said, laughing boyishly. "Dangerous mean . . . I want to know. Dangerous always make me want to know."

She shifted grounds. "Where is your wife?"

"She work. She work in Shanghai."

Norma coughed. "You mean, she isn't even here?" He shook his head. "And your children?"

"In school. He will be home four o'clock." He looked quickly about him. "My mother and father, they work, too. All come home four o'clock." She examined her watch: it was 3:30. She had to get out of there. She stood up and pulled on her jacket. "Do not worry," he said, nonchalantly. "The old man at the gate, he tell my mother and father I come here with *waiguoren*." He smiled sadly.

"Aren't you afraid?"

"No," he said. A note of defiance broke through. He studied her for a moment and said: "I want visit you at Youyi Binguan."

She was startled. "No," she said, quickly, "that will not be possible."

"Why?"

She said it. They had gone much too far for her to play the game any longer. "Because you will get into trouble."

He did not touch her. Chinese men did not touch foreign women they had just met and brought home to their empty apartments. But he did the next best thing. He spoke to her and tried to frame the words in a language he held in his arms like a baby.

"I must see you again," he said. "I must."

The soldiers at the Chairman's tomb led her to the front of the mile-long queue as if she were some important state guest, and she shuffled up the steps beside a woman her own age.

The two of them exchanged glances as they walked into the marble lobby. Norma went right because she had heard that the Chairman's left ear was rotting. But when she arrived at the catafalque and peered down into the glass box, she was disappointed to discover it was just like a wax ear— lifeless, a mere reproduction, an appendage Madame Tussaud herself would have admired— and then she was propelled out again, down the steps and into the square before the massive Qianmen gate. She felt suddenly disoriented. It was more than being lost. It occurred to her that, although she could live in this country for fifty years and yet be seen as a *waiguoren*, a foreigner, an alien, there was nonetheless something to all this. Something strong and honest and good.

She was, in fact, surprised to see Youmei. He called her from the hotel gate because Chinese people were still out-of-bounds when they walked into any part of their country where foreigners congregated. She went to the window and watched him walk up the steps and hand his pass to the *fuwuyuan* who watched him. In the time it took him to walk the stairs and knock upon her door, she had seen the *fuwuyuan* run across the small park to the office to report that a comrade had gone to visit the Canadian lady.

She let Youmei through the door, and he gave her a box of chocolates and a small book of Chinese poems in English. A lover would not have done more. They sat together and drank tea, and he practiced his English upon her. But it was more than English she heard. It was that second voice she heard again, the one down under the bright one, and it was more like a cry of pain from a proud man.

"Youmei," she said, "what do you do?"

"Nothing," he said. "I sit in office all day. I do nothing."

"What would you like to do?"

He thought for a moment and said, "Pardon?"

"What would you like to do?"

"I do not know. I do not know nothing. I want to know . . . something. I want to know . . . about the world." He looked into her eyes in a way no other Chinese man had ever done. "I want you tell me. What is it like? The world. What is it like?"

"I . . . don't know anything about it."

"But you come from Canada!"

"I don't know anything about Canada, but I will tell you something about China. Just as soon as you came into the building, the *fuwuyuan* went directly to the office. What are they afraid of? Are you afraid of them?"

"They are afraid. But I am not afraid," he said. He was much too calm. She was the one who was frightened. "I am not afraid of anyone."

Later, she tried to recall what he had said after that, but it was gone. She was still suffering from shock. It was as if something inside her had died. All she remembered was that they had talked for some time, said foolish words and laughed together, perhaps too loudly, and when it was time for him to leave, they had got to their feet and she had taken him by the hand as they walked toward the door. He tripped on her rug and held onto her for just a moment, and, when they regained their balance and laughed, he had looked at her again and she had figured in any other situation he would have kissed her, but Youmei had only reddened. Still, she had clung to his hand as she opened the door . . . and it was then that she saw the *fuwuyuan.*

The girl was in the act of delivering envelopes and newspapers to her door, but at the moment she was less interested in delivering mail than in noting that the two of them were holding hands and laughing intimately.

The foreign woman and the Chinese man.

Norma rode back through Tian'anmen and down into Chang An until she arrived at the ornate, golden archway of Zhongnanhai. She stopped to take a picture of it, but the day was too dark. Ah, well! she had to get used to the dark. She had to learn once more how to survive the stygian underground garage where she buried her car every night. She had to remember how to turn off the key and sit for a moment with the lights off to study all the caves and crevices where they lurked. She had to practice jumping quickly from the car and locking it, rushing across the open spaces and into the elevator, riding up to the dark corridor, along to her doorway, making sure that they weren't following her. She had to learn how to dig her keys from her purse and unlock the door, flick on the light, check the rooms and the window locks, and only then, after all that, perhaps she could relax. She could make herself a stiff drink and take a hot shower and watch the evening news, usually serial scenes of rape and bloodshed and murder, and then the severe comedies and late, late shows until she could collapse into her cold highly- starched bed.

Alone.